I0725290

THE HOUSEWIFE ASSASSIN'S ANTISOCIAL MEDIA TIPS

JOSIE BROWN

A BOOK BY

SIGNAL PRESS

ONE OF MANY GREAT SIGNAL PRESS BOOKS

San Francisco, CA

Library of Congress Cataloging-in-Publication Data is available upon request

Cover Design by Andrew Brown, ClickTwiceDesign.com

Trade Paperback ISBN: 978-1-970093-30-8

Hardcover ISBN: 978-1-970093-35-3

V022422

after a long day. I can't wait to read the next in the series. Highly Recommended!"

—*CrimeThrillerGirl.com*

"This was an addictive read–gritty but funny at the same time. I ended up reading it in just one evening and couldn't go to sleep until I knew what the outcome would be! It was action-packed and humorous from the start, and that continued throughout, I was pleased to discover that this is the first of a series and look forward to getting my hands on Book Two so I can see where life takes Donna and her family next!"

—*Me, My Books, and I*

"The two halves of Donna's life make sense. As you follow her story, there's no point where you think of her as "Assassin Donna" vs. "Mummy Donna', her attitude to life is even throughout. I really like how well this is done. And as for Jack. I'll have one of those, please?"

—*The Northern Witch's Book Blog*

Novels in The Housewife Assassin Series

The Housewife Assassin's Handbook

(Book 1)

The Housewife Assassin's Guide to Gracious Killing

(Book 2)

The Housewife Assassin's Killer Christmas Tips

(Book 3)

The Housewife Assassin's Relationship Survival Guide

(Book 4)

The Housewife Assassin's Vacation to Die For

(Book 5)

The Housewife Assassin's Recipes for Disaster

(Book 6)

The Housewife Assassin's Hollywood Scream Play

(Book 7)

The Housewife Assassin's Killer App

(Book 8)

The Housewife Assassin's Hostage Hosting Tips

(Book 9)

The Housewife Assassin's Garden of Deadly Delights

(Book 10)

Social Media

How social is social media?

Well, that depends on who you are, why you're on, and where you post it.

For example: if you want to show off the cake you've just baked, post it on Instagram.

(Word of caution: before posting, take a quick tour of the platform using such hashtags as #cake or #dessert or #sweets to make sure your culinary gem is staged and lit as appetizingly as Insta's usual eye candy. Otherwise, no comment literally means "No comment.")

Want to humble-brag on your children? Facebook is the platform for you! You can show off to your heart's content. (Reality check: are your friends' offspring even more accomplished? Whether the answer is a grudging "Yes" or a relieved "Hell, no..." be prepared to thumbs up the photos your friends post as well. Otherwise, they may give tit for tat. (Again, in this case, silence is not golden.)

Now, if you want to rant about the lousy disservice you

received at a particular chain store, Twitter is where you post it. The store will certainly see it and reach out to you publicly —

But then follow up with nothing that resolves the problem. Why should it? It's one measly tweet. Is that proof they feel your pain?

NOT.

Which shows you just how antisocial media is. Tweeting or posting—even creating a silly TikTok video—may give you a few seconds of satisfaction, but in the end it tallies up to nothing of real worth, let alone satisfying actions.

Instead, get out on the street and wave at someone. Or knock on a neighbor's door with that cake. Better yet, write a letter to an old friend, enclosing those photos of your children.

The ripple effect may take your message much further, and the response you get back will mean much more to you.

Especially if it's accompanied with a smile.

IT'S TWO-THIRTY IN THE MORNING AND I'D RATHER BE anywhere but behind the counter at Granny Doo's Diner on the desolate, godforsaken corner of US-395 and Searles Station Road.

In other words, I'm out in the middle of nowhere: the Mojave Desert to be exact, and fifteen miles as the crow flies to the Naval Air Weapons Station in China Lake, California.

Frankly, you won't see any crows in this neck of the desert. They know better than to fly over the Naval Air Base, and for good reason: they'd get wiped out by an air fleet of F-16s programmed with Artificial Intelligence.

Nowadays, every maneuver—be it air combat, reconnaissance, mission planning, or logistics—is foolproof.

It's DARPA tech wizardry at its finest.

And no other country has anything similar—

Which is why one of the base's mechanics—a guy named Winston Pettigrew—put out feelers to the Chinese to see if they'd want an SD card containing our swarm warfare technology. Winston's job is to load the software onto the fleet's cockpit computers. At some point, he downloaded it to sell to the highest bidder.

Of course, China leaped at the chance to get its hands on it.

Luckily, our pals the South Koreans intercepted Winston's coded negotiations. They handed it off to an asset who works for my employer—the US Government-sanctioned black ops organization, Acme Industries—so that both South Korea and the US can claim no knowledge of foiling China's scheme.

That's where I come in. Winston arranged for the hand-off to take place here, at Granny Doo's. When the time comes—tonight, in fact—I'll be conducting some sleight of hand: swapping Winston's card for one of our own, which is embedded with a trojan that will release faulty algorithms when the US deems fit, and crash China's air fleet.

After Winston's contacts go on their merry way with the wrong SD card, Jack and I will arrest the seller and destroy the card holding the stolen intel.

Rest her soul, Granny Doo is long gone—but not far off. Just to Palm Springs. With the payout of a seven-million-dollar Lotto ticket, she bought a mansion built in the middle of a whole lot of sand, and a few cabana boys to boot. She gifted the diner to her nephew, Bucky Doolittle, who is the diner's short-order cook. When I applied for the waitressing job, Bucky—a sunburned sixty-something desert rat—looked me up and down (breast to thigh, anyway) and candidly declared, "You'll do just fine as the overnight counter cutie. The shift begins at midnight and runs for eight hours. You'll make ten bucks per, plus whatever tips you can wangle out of the tight-assed truckers who stop in here."

"No, sir," I said. "You'll pay me minimum wage, just as the state of California mandates."

To make my point, I smacked my bubble gum so hard that Bucky ducked. I suppose he thought one of the sixteen-wheelers rumbling down the road had popped a tire.

He must have liked my giggle—more than likely, he liked the way my breasts jiggled when I guffawed—because he grudgingly told me I had the gig.

Lucky me.

He had no choice. No one else had applied. Acme made sure of that by scrubbing the job notice from the closest Craig's List feed.

Since setting the date, Winston has shown up a couple of times. Frankly, I think he chose this place because its lousy food ensures that he and his contact will be left the only ones in the joint. The first time Winston came in, he nursed a cup of coffee and took a bite of his pie and almost gagged.

My boss, Ryan Clancy, was so worried that Bucky's rancid cardboard-crust pies would give Winston a case of the runs and that the traitor would choose another drop location that he begged me to bake homemade pies for the diner. At first, Bucky was reticent to take me up on my offer. But after I whipped up one of my apple pies and served it to him, he quickly changed his mind.

"It's like heaven with a golden-brown crust," he sighed.

"Is that a tear in your eye?" I asked.

He nodded, then honked his nose into a paper napkin. "What can I say? I'm sentimental."

"Do you mean to tell me that Granny Doo's pies were once this good?"

He snorted at that. "Nope. She always bought 'em at Costco."

I didn't have the nerve to ask Bucky where he gets *his* pies.

The next time Winston showed up, I gave him a large wedge of my chocolate pecan on the house, just to assure him it was edible. I could tell by his shit-eating grin that he liked it.

Or maybe he appreciated the way my breasts peeked out from my push-up bra when I bent down to refill his coffee. Does it matter what keeps him coming back for more? Nah. Not when our national security is at risk.

Winston is here now. He walked in just an hour ago, scanned the diner, then took his usual seat: the third counter stool on the left. It's the furthest away from the big screen TV hanging over the grill: a suggestion I made to Bucky on my second day at work. "It'll keep the patrons in their stools," I predicted.

He now grudgingly agrees I was right, again.

The cheapskate jerry-rigged the TV with a rope that runs from the wall to a couple of unanchored ceiling hooks, so that it is tilted. "That way, the bar customers don't get a crick in their necks," Bucky explained.

"You're asking for trouble with that set-up," I countered. "I wouldn't be surprised if the vibrations from one of the big rigs flying by this rickety shack send it crashing down on your head one of these days."

Some twenty minutes ago, two truckers sauntered in before Winston. They're sitting at the counter a few stools away, directly under the TV. They seem transfixed by a replay of the Giants pummeling the Dodgers.

A third trucker—my mission partner and husband, Jack —drove up after Winston. Jack now sports some chin scruff and a retro Salty Crew trucker's cap that's a bona fide for those who drive Mack Anthems tricked out with a 70-inch sleeper. Like me, he's also equipped with earbuds and contact lenses that allow us eyes and ears, controlled by the rest of our mission team, who are working out of the back of the Mack.

Acme's ace tech op, Arnie Locklear, is monitoring the security cams I placed strategically throughout the diner while Bucky snored in the cot in the pantry. And our cutout-slash-cleaner-slash "save our asses best he can" operative, Abu Nagashahi, is doing reconnaissance while waiting to see if we'll need any clean-ups on Aisle Five.

Arnie's wife—Emma Honeycutt, who is also Acme's Communications Intelligence Director—is just an earbud away from the rest of us. In case something goes awry and takes us far afield, she'll relay any SATCOM visuals, using the diner as Ground Zero.

Odds are that this mission will go as smoothly as the coffee I'm now serving: my own blend of Excelsa and

Robusta. Bucky's been tickled pink that it's a hit with patrons.

Jack took the last stool on the left, which is just two away from our target and the closest to the restrooms and pantry. To keep Winston from suspecting us, other than placing his order for burgers, fries, and a Ginger Ale, Jack ignores me.

Frankly, I think he's going a step too far. I mean, come on already. The only one who *wouldn't* be leering at me in this much-too-tight waitress uniform would have to be a castrated monk.

A half-hour after Winston showed up, a tow-headed ice blue-eyed couple—twentyish and glamping in a tricked-out Silver Bullet Airstream—came in to shake the dust off their lean, tanned bodies before plopping down in one of the diner's booths. After ordering coffee and a large order of fries, they've been charging their computers and phones on the diner's new USB charging stations and electrical outlet strips now built into every booth. Using our free WIFI, they've been uploading a stash of photos to the newest must-use social media platform, FaceStaTweet.

The chargers and outlets were also my idea. When I pointed out to Bucky that these amenities would encourage patrons to sit and nosh even longer—perhaps even make it a must-stop destination—he crowed with delight. "Well, aren't you a little smartie pants!"

I smiled, then gave Abu the order to install them. I figure that the best quid pro quo is hooking up Jack's Mack to the diner's power supply.

So far, none of the diner's patrons have approached Winston, nor has he interacted with anyone. And yet, he's as skittish as a peekapoo that's been left on the shoulder of the expressway in the dark.

Why would that be? Certainly, it's not about the money. Half of Winston's crypto-cash payment has already been transferred into his designated account. (Not really; Arnie hacked and then jacked it).

I'm now pulling three fresh-baked pies out of the oven behind the diner's counter: apple with a lattice crust, cherry, and pecan. The fragrant smell of hot fruit and baked crust wafts through the air. Noses quiver. One of the truckers is drooling. While the pies cool, I saunter over to each patron and offer refills from the fresh pot of coffee in my hand. I'm not surprised that everyone has a pie request. I suppose they're anxious to cut the grease left in their guts by Bucky's cheeseburgers.

One of the truckers at the counter wants cherry. The other goes for pecan. The Glamping Gal wants an apple slice, while Glamping Guy requests cherry.

Winston wants apple.

Jack requests a slice of the cherry pie, for good reason: when Winston's guest appears, I'll deliver Jack's pie to Winston, which will give me an excuse for a little sleight-of-hand. If I'm successful, I'll have swapped Winston's SD card with the one in my apron pocket.

Except for Jack and Winston, I've just set the other patrons' pie slices and tabs in front of them when the front door chimes. A tall block of a man wearing a cowboy hat looks around, then takes a stool two away from Winston, on his right.

Hmmm…

Suddenly, I hear Emma's voice in my ear. I wish I could say she's coming in loud and clear, but she's not.

Jack is frowning. Apparently, he's also trying to make out what she's saying through all the static.

I keep my eye on Winston. I know Jack is doing the same. If this is when the handoff takes place, we can't afford to be distracted.

Cowboy takes off his ten-gallon and places it on the stool beside Winston. "That pecan pie sure smells good, ma'am! How 'bout a piece of that with some java?" His drawl is as thick as molasses and just as sweet.

I'm glad he doesn't want a burger instead. Bucky has snuck out back to call Granny Doo and plead with her for a loan since the wad he bet on the Dodgers looks like it'll wipe him out.

I grin coyly at Cowboy. "Be right with you, mister," I say, as I cut Jack a slice of the cherry.

Then I cut a wedge of apple pie for Winston—

But I give it to Jack instead.

Winston is too busy eyeing Cowboy to notice I haven't handed him his pie of choice. A moment later, Cowboy nonchalantly asks him: "Isn't the Ridgecrest Gun Range around here somewhere?"

Nervously, Winston mutters, "East of here, on Brown Road. The other side of three-ninety-five, at the junction." He then reaches into his pocket. He's palming something:

An SD card.

So, that was the passcode.

I must turn my back as I cut Cowboy's slice of pecan pie. But I'm facing a mirrored wall, so I can still see

Winston as he slips the card under the rim of the plate in front of him.

At that moment, Jack stands up and leans over toward Winston, the apple pie plate in his hand. "Hey, dude, I think this pie was meant for you, and you got mine instead."

In a flash, I pull the trojan-laden SD card from my pocket. Turning around, I coo, "Goodness, you're right! So sorry!" With a giggle and a smile, I take Winston's plate—and the card under it—and hand them to Jack.

Even before the plate of apple pie is placed on the counter, I've slipped the trojan-embedded SD card under it.

Winston is suspicious enough to slide his new plate over about an inch. Satisfied that the card is still there, he waits until I turn back around to cut a piece of the pecan before he slips it under the man's hat.

"Coffee too, please, ma'am," Cowboy's command comes with a chuckle. He's playing it cool: flirting, taking his time.

Not too long, I hope. I've had enough of this hellhole diner in the desert. I'm ready to wrap up this mission and go home to my nice, warm bed—with Jack.

Oh, darn, the coffee pot is empty. I'll need a new bag of my coffee mix. I crouch down and open the bottom drawer where it's kept. Before I can stand up. I hear Winston give a long sigh of relief—

Make that his last gasp. His life drains out of him as a bullet propels him facedown into his apple pie. His arms dangle over the counter, slapping me on the head.

I hear the whisper of a suppressor. The next thing I

know, Cowboy's brains splatter the grill. He too flops onto the counter. I swallow hard so as not to gag when I see what's seeping out of the gaping hole in his head.

Through the convex security mirror hanging in the corner, I watch as the glamping couple move toward the counter. Each sports a Sig Sauer.

The slight sigh of their guns' suppressors comes a second before the death grunts of the two truckers who'd been watching the baseball game. They too slump onto the counter, victims of being in the wrong place at the wrong time.

Oh my God—

Where is Jack?

No time for fear. Not now, as Glamper Guy strolls over to dearly departed Cowboy. At the same time, he growls, "Instead of grabbing souvenirs from the dead dudes' pockets, find out what happened to the waitress and the trucker who was at the end of the counter."

"Don't worry about them. She's probably in the middle of polishing his knob in the men's room. Can't say I blame her. He's adorable." Glamper Girl giggles. "Maybe that's how she makes her tips." As she pilfers their bodies, the wallets of the dead truckers slap the counter. "Ha! Imagine their faces when they come out and see this slaughter!"

"They're not coming out because we're going to shoot them. We don't need witnesses who can ID us. But hey, whattaya say we have some fun with them first? You know, make them perform for us, like a live porn show." Glamper Guy grunts as he shoves Cowboy to one side. "Jeez, this dude is so damn heavy that I can't move him to get to his pockets!"

"I don't get why watching makes you hotter than doin' the dirty yourself!" Glamper Gal huffs. As her voice gets closer, I squeeze myself as far under the counter as I can get. I'm next to the trash can. The smell is vile.

The only benefit is that I'm located directly across from the grill, where Bucky has left his meat cleaver. I'd grab it but Glamper Girl is right over me, rifling through Winston's jacket. "Tell you what: we'll kill her first, and then I'll do it with him. At least, he'll go out with a smile on his face… Ha! I found it—under the dude's ten-gallon!"

The SD card with the trojan.

Our boss, Ryan Clancy at Acme, will bust a gut if I let them take it.

Something is sizzling on the grill. Aw heck! Bucky had put up a skillet of grits before he walked out to make his call.

I leap up and grab the skillet. Then with both hands, I wallop Glamper Girl in the face with it.

Scalded, she lets loose with a bloodcurdling scream before stumbling backward. Slipping on Winston's blood, she falls. Her head hits the concrete floor. Her eyes are still open, but blood makes a damp red halo around head.

As I turn to pick up the cleaver, Glamper Guy leaps over the counter. His gun is pointed right at me. "What say you put that down, nice and easy?" he snarls. "Then get on your knees like a good girl 'cause there's something I'd like you to do to me too, just as nice, and just as easy."

I nod meekly. Slowly, I take the cleaver in my hand—

And chop the rope holding the television set—

Sending it crashing on top of Glamper Guy.

He falls backward, dazed, dropping his gun on the grill.

Stumbling forward, he reaches for it.

Wielding the cleaver with both hands, I chop his wrist.

Glamper Guy falls to the floor. But his hand, still holding the gun, sizzles on the red-hot grill.

The smell of burnt flesh churns my stomach. Even worse are his howls as the blood drains from him.

His last breath is a death rattle.

Relieved, I collapse against a cabinet.

Jack and Abu burst through the diner's front door. Eyes opened wide, they take in the massacre.

I stare at Jack. "Where the hell did you go?"

"I slipped out the back to give the SD card to Arnie," he explains. "Then I put a tracker on Cowboy's car." He stares down at Glamper Girl. "From the looks of things, it was a waste of time. I take it they were robbing the joint?"

"Yes…No! More than that…" Still confused, I shake my head. "I mean…They shot Winston and Cowboy first."

"Just based on Cowboy's size, I would have done the same," Abu admits.

"But that's not all. When she found the SD card under his hat, she said, 'I found it.' So, maybe they were assets for a country that lost out on Winston's offer?"

"Wrong guess," declares Jack. He's kneeling beside Glamper Girl. "Look here."

Glamper Girl landed on the floor with her legs sprawled apart. Her fashionably frayed denim short shorts are pulled up high enough to reveal her thigh. She sports a tattoo of a snake wrapped around an eagle.

Abu whistles. "Ah, hell. *Orel i Zmeya.*"

Translated from Russian: Eagle and Snake, which is the name of an international terrorist organization made up of soldiers of fortune who have been burned or retired from military intelligence groups from around the world.

Oh, what fun. In our last run-in with this rogue organization, they'd planted a bomb in our house.

We hear the back door close. A moment later, Bucky saunters in. The sight of all the carnage stops him cold in his tracks. When his eyes roll back to me, he whispers, *"What the hell happened?"*

"A fight broke out when I announced we were out of the apple pie." I shrug. "Not to worry. The cops are on their way."

Bucky backs away. "Are you kidding me? I've got to get out of here! The sheriff is my bookie and he'll kill me if I don't have his cut."

He's out the door in a flash.

Abu sighs. "You guys take off. Emma already called the Feds. Arnie and I will stick around and explain. We've been instructed to dispose of Winston but to bring in Cowboy and the campers. Afterward, Arnie will drive their Silverstream back to Acme. I'll do the same with Cowboy's car. Forensics will be going over them with a fine-tooth comb for clues."

I take off my apron. "If Bucky ever gets back, tell him I've quit."

Abu snickers. "I doubt that'll be the case." He brightens. "Which means Granny Doo will probably put this joint up for sale. Because of your pies, news of this place is traveling fast in the trucker community. Hey, what do you think about going in as partners? With your pies and my knowledge of franchise management, we'll be a conglomerate in no time!"

"I'd invest in that," Arnie declares. "What do you say, Donna?"

I shake my head as I stroll out the door.

Sputtering with laughter, Jack is on my heels.

As we head out toward the Mack, I hold out my hand to him. "Hey, can I drive?"

"Like hell!" he exclaims. "Ryan's going to be angry enough that the swap was never made. What do you think he'd do to us if you crashed the Mack?"

I get it. Arnie and Abu are already burying one body in the desert: Winston's. No need to make it three.

2

Sentiment Analysis

Specifically regarding social media, sentiment analysis *tools detect whether customer feedback is positive, negative, neutral, or nil toward a piece of text. Over time, by taking an average of all social media interactions, SM marketers can gauge the general mood of their audience.*

Every time you open your mouth, you are doing your own form of sentiment analysis—albeit not always successfully. Case in point: You sweetly ask your husband to mow the lawn. He says "Sure, in a moment." (Analysis: neutral.)

Three hours later, though you've asked him again and again in ever-increasingly agitated tones, he is still sitting in front of the boob tube, thus allowing the device to live up to that unfortunate moniker. (Analysis: nil.)

Perhaps you should check his pulse.

If he is still breathing and yet still oblivious to your blatant messaging despite all the signals you've given, then perhaps positive sentiment analysis will best be achieved via a bullet blasting through his eighty-five-inch 4K UHD HDR 32X TV monitor.

(If I'm right, positive reviews are welcomed.)

~

"MOM...*MOM!*" MY OLDEST CHILD, MARY, IS HISSING IN my ear.

"Go away," I grunt.

In truth, I'm glad to have been wakened from my nightmare. In it, I'm still at Granny Doo's Diner. A snake is crawling out from under Cowboy's ten-gallon and an eagle is making its lunch from the hole in his skull, despite my attempt to tempt both creatures out the door with one of my pies. Who doesn't like tart apple spiced with cinnamon in a golden buttery crust, anyway?...

I wonder what my shrink, Dr. Hartley, would say to this dark dream?

"Okay, if you insist on sleeping in, so be it." Mary sighs deeply. "I'm grabbing the car to drive Jeff and Trisha to school."

"Don't talk crazy!" I pop up from under my comforter to find myself facing her as well as the rest of my beloved brood—my son, Jeff, my younger daughter, Trisha, and my Aunt Phyllis.

Phyllis nudges Mary. "See? I told you that threat would work."

Mary scowls—not at Aunt Phyllis. At me. "Won't you ever forgive me for the fender-bender I made while you gave me defensive driving lessons?"

"The fact that you refer to pulling out of the driveway

while chatting on your cell phone as 'defensive driving' speaks volumes as to why your parents now suffer from facial tics," I retort.

Mary frowns. "Well…Dad *never* makes faces when I drive."

I poke the mound of manhood sleeping beside me. "Go ahead, big guy. Tell her the truth: that you were scared witless."

Groaning, Jack takes the pillow off his head. Wearily, he bleats: "I plead the fifth."

"I'll ignore that," Mary huffs, "but only because I've got some *really great news.*"

"Hold on, let's give them a choice." Jeff opens his arms wide in our direction. "Mr. and Mrs. Craig, which would you prefer first—the good news, the bad news, or the worst news?"

Eyes now wide open, Jack and I look at each other. "Your call, Mrs. Craig," Jack murmurs.

I sigh. "Let's start with something pleasant."

Mary squeals. "Well, then, you'll be happy to know that —*drum roll, please!*—I've been chosen as the valedictorian of my graduating class!"

"Wow!" Yes, I'm stunned, but not surprised. In the past year, Mary has gone from being a headstrong party girl to a serious young adult. She's not just concerned about the world's problems but determined to make it a better place. She was inspired by our dear friend, Mario Martinez, a US intelligence officer who works as the liaison between the White House and the Director of National Intelligence— another close pal of Acme and the Craigs, Marcus Branham.

Will this goal put her on my path of spy versus spy? Frankly, I hope she never goes out into the field. But if she does, Jack and I will do everything we can to prepare her for the worst-case scenarios, of which there are many. Her training starts immediately after graduation.

That is, if Orel i Zmeya doesn't foil our plans for a serene summer. It would be great to take a few months off from saving the world from its villains.

I pull Mary in close so that I can give her a kiss. "Congratulations, darling. I am so, so proud of you!"

Mary smiles bashfully. "No one was more surprised than me."

Jeff snickers. "I was."

Mary picks up one of my slippers and hurls it at him–

But Jeff catches it, then shoots it back—

Only to have Trisha snatch it in mid-air before it meets its target: Mary's head.

Once we've recovered from our collective shock, everyone exclaims: "Great catch!"

Trisha shrugs. "*Hello*, everyone? I'm on the county's Soccer A-Team, remember? And let's not forget that I've learned from the best." She throws the slipper so quickly that Jeff isn't ready when it hits him soundly on the noggin.

"You're welcome." Jeff is teasing, but he's also proud of the role he's played in Trisha's growth as an athlete.

She sticks out her tongue at him. "I meant Dominic. Remember that summer we moved in with him?"

"How could we forget," Jack mutters. "Ah, good times."

He's joking. It's never a good time when the Feds

surround your home because they are mistakenly under the assumption that you're America's Most Wanted Fugitives Numbers One and Two. We got out, but only after blowing our house sky high, in the hope of fooling them that we'd died. After our names were cleared, we bunked at Dominic's, who lives around the corner.

(That way, the kids could stay in Hilldale's great school district while our home was rebuilt. Always the top priority, right?)

"I watched all that English football with Dominic," Trisha explains. "He taught me how to kick a soccer ball. Every now and then, he shows up at my games."

I feel a rash of guilt creeping up my neck. Whereas Jeff's basketball games are in the evening, Trisha's soccer games are in the afternoon—usually when I'm in the middle of some act of derring-do. Sure, it's great that Aunt Phyllis is there to pick up the slack. But it's not the same.

As Mary moves on to college, Trisha is entering middle school. I make a silent vow to be present and accounted for this very precious time in her life.

"Now that we've gotten the good stuff out of the way, why don't we move on to the less pleasant news?" Jack suggests.

"A picture—or, in this case, a FaceStaTweet video—is worth a thousand words." Trisha crawls into bed between Jack and me. Pulling her phone out of her pocket, she taps it. A video begins:

Aunt Phyllis is dancing. We're not talking a jitterbug or the Watusi. It's hip-hop, and boy is it hot.

She's jamming. She's greasy. She's hittin' it *hard*. She's bustin' moves.

When she *throws it back,* my mouth drops open.

Aunt Phyllis grabs Trisha's cell phone. Squinting at the screen, she exclaims, "Hey…that's me!" If her smile was any wider, you'd have thought she'd won at Lotto.

Awed, Jack declares, "That last bit would make a back-up dancer for Beyoncé blush!"

Trisha nods vehemently. "She does it whenever I make a soccer goal!"

"You bet I do!" Aunt Phyllis chucks Trisha's cheek. "Only my little sweetie deserves Phyllis's Get-Down dance!"

"Is that what you call it?" Jack laughs so hard that I smother him with a pillow to make him hush.

"The team loves it. Don't they, baby?" Phyllis looks at Trisha for backup.

Through gritted teeth, Trisha mutters, "Oh, yeah. Believe me, they can't talk of anything else."

"Boo-yah!" My aunt's fist pump sends her to her knees. She springs up just as fast. "I've got a few new grooves to practice before tomorrow's game. Gotta go! Porter has the morning off. He's taking me out for breakfast. But I'll be at practice to pick you up later today, Trisha, so don't you worry." She moon-walks out of the room.

"I won't," Trisha murmurs under her breath.

"Who took the video?" I ask.

"It might have been Mr. Chiffray. He comes to all of Janie's games."

"Figures," Jack huffs.

"He would have done it for Porter because he loves it when she dances. You know how Porter feels about her." Trisha blushes. "But Mr. Chiffray's Secret Service detail isn't allowed to use their cell phones while they guard him, except for security purposes."

Now that Lee is no longer our nation's president, he's made it a point to devote as much time as possible to his children. Janie is his stepdaughter. Her mother, his now deceased wife, Babette, was the widow of Jonah Breck: a member of the Quorum, a group of powerful men who fronted terrorist organizations all over the world to suit their financial and political agendas. Jonah was killed by my terrorist ex-husband, Carl, before he could make a deal with the Feds over his wrongdoings.

Babette met Lee when he purchased Jonah's conglomerate. Lee's toddler son, Harrison, is the product of Babette's affair with Salem Rahmin al-Sadah, another Quorum financier.

Do you see a pattern here?

Oh yeah, I guess it's worth mentioning that Lee has an unrequited crush on me, which is why Jack just grins and bears it when Lee is around.

Quickly, Trisha adds, "Or it could have been one of the other parents who posted it somewhere."

Gently, I ask, "Trisha, does Aunt Phyllis's dance embarrass you enough to make you hesitate before making a goal?"

Trisha grimaces. "At first...well, yeah, I was embarrassed. But Coach Kendra talked me off that ledge. She reminded me that Aunt Phyllis only does it because she's proud of me." She sighs. "And besides, everyone else seems to love it—my teammates, their parents..." Her voice trails off.

"You know she'd stop if she knew it embarrassed you," I point out.

Trisha thinks for a moment, then attempts a smile. "Let's not make a big deal out of it. At least, not yet."

I pull her close for a kiss. "Okay, so now that we've gotten two of the items off the family business agenda, what's the third thing that needs our undivided attention?"

"Trisha is making breakfast!" Jeff rolls his eyes.

"Why...I think that's wonderful," I proclaim. *Trisha cooks?*

From the look on Jack's face, he's just as surprised at this turn of events as me. "So...when did you start donning your mother's apron?" he asks our youngest.

"When the rest of us thought we'd starve to death because you're always away on missions," Jeff grumbles.

"What, you don't know how to crack an egg?" I retort. "Mary, I know you do."

Mary's cheeks pink up. "While you were away, Aunt Phyllis took Jeff and Trisha to school because I've been going into Hilldale High early and staying late."

"How come?" Jack asks.

"Mario has offered me a White House internship over the summer—with your permission, of course." Mary smiles hopefully. "He's given me some training assignments. I've been getting up early to complete them, as well as working on them after school."

I force a smile on my lips. "Your determination is impressive."

"So is the assignment—if I get it." Mary lifts her head proudly.

Trisha snickers, "Evan will be disappointed."

Mary's boyfriend, Evan Martin, is also Jack's and my ward. In my youth, his father, Robert, and I were friends in high school. Sadly, his mother, Catherine, was jealous of our relationship and used it to ruin my reputation. Robert became a tech entrepreneur, whereas Catherine became a U.S. Congressperson. When she campaigned for the U.S. presidency, I was assigned to protect her. She ended up being a traitor: both to our country and to her husband, whom she had murdered (by my rat-bastard terrorist first husband, Carl) because Robert discovered her deceit and threatened to divorce her. Evan brought her dual duplicity to light.

Though Catherine won the presidency, she was never sworn in. Instead, she was sent to prison for sanctioning Robert's murder. Ironically, she was killed before she could confess on the record to being an asset for the terrorist group, the Quorum.

Lee, the Vice-President Elect, became president—which made Babette his First Lady.

The fact that she was a Quorum asset complicated things. But all that's in the past, right?

"Evan will just have to understand." Mary declares. "If you love someone, yes, counsel them. But you must also support their decisions."

Jack and I trade wide-eyed glances. We must be thinking the same thing: our oldest child has indeed grown up.

I kiss Trisha's cheek. "If you need a sous chef, I'm here for you."

Trisha shakes her head. "I've got it covered. I'll holler when it's ready." She's out the door in a flash.

Jack picks up his cell and frowns. "We'd better hurry too. We're due at the office in an hour. Ryan will be waiting to debrief us."

Something tells me it'll be more like a dressing-down for our mission going awry.

Ah well, can't win them all.

As I tumble out of bed, I wag my finger at Jeff. "You've got to quit teasing Trisha about her cooking."

He snickers. "You'd do the same if you'd choked on one of her dry muffins."

"Practice makes perfect," I point out.

Jack nods. "And she's got a great teacher."

He's right. Some time together in the kitchen, testing recipes, will make for great mother-daughter bonding. With Mary moving onto college, I need it as much as Trisha.

They grow up too quickly.

Life is too short.

3

Fomo

EVERYONE WANTS TO FEEL AS IF THEY ARE A PART OF something. If that "something" is happening on social media, the acronym, FOMO, describes it aptly: "fear of missing out."

For example:

On Twitter, if you don't check your feed often enough, others will think you're only interested in you, yourself, and thou; that you couldn't care less about what's happening in the rest of the world, be it popular trends, up-to-the-minute news, or political turmoil.

On Facebook, if you skip enough posts, you fear that people will think you don't have a life.

On Instagram, if you don't post artistically, they will think your life lacks great style.

On TikTok, if you don't post while dancing to the latest Taylor Swift hit, your few viewers there will think you aren't fun.

So, here's the deal:

Plan A: Buck up and do all of this. So what if you don't end *up with a million followers! Even if you do, trying to reach the second million will leave you where you are today: depressed, unable to get out of bed, lying in the fetal position with the covers pulled over your head.*

Then there's Plan B: Let the social media train pass you by.

Instead, go out and live the life you want—without posting it anywhere. Take a language course. Sit in on an art lecture. Watch a bee suckle an open bloom. Listen to a gurgling creek. Stare up at the clouds as they glide lazily through the sky.

It's called JOMO. (Joy of Missing Out.)

Your life can't always be summed up in a 140-character tweet. It's an open book with many pages still to write.

"I GUESS YOU KNOW WHAT I'M GOING TO SAY," RYAN GROWLS.

Our mission team—Arnie, Emma, and Abu—which is already assembled in the conference room with Acme's CEO, stays silent. Even Arnie realizes that this is no time to crack a joke.

Lucky Dominic has gotten a reprieve from Ryan's gripe session. Even if we'd planted him behind the grill doing short-order duty, his posh demeanor would have stood out like a sore thumb among the truckers.

And besides, no way would he have donned a hairnet.

The look on Ryan's face is easy to read. "You cocked things up! The Director of National Intelligence wanted the Chinese operative captured alive and kicking, the guy you call…" Ryan looks down at our summary statement, then looks up again, if only to roll his eyes in disgust: "'Ten Gallon.' And since he conveniently has no fingerprints and a mouthful of untraceable implants, I guess we'll keep calling him that."

"In all fairness, sir, we had no intel that Eagle and Snake was going to show up at our little hootenanny and that they'd blow his brains out all over the diner," Jack points out.

"We brought back his vehicle," Abu adds. "Was forensics able to come up with any leads?"

Ryan frowns. "Not a thing. The license plate was stolen and all identifying markings on the vehicle's parts were conveniently scrubbed."

"Give us some credit," Jack implores him. "Not only did we secure the intel but rid the universe of two soldiers of fortune, a Chinese operative, and a traitor to our country."

Ryan snorts. "Don't be so cocky, Mr. Craig. The other half of the mission was to plant the trojan within the Chinese military's database, remember? Trust me, Marcus Branham isn't doing cartwheels over this outcome." Still, he nods grudgingly in my direction. "Donna, you were right about one thing: the campers weren't just on a random murder-robbery spree. They were Eagle and Snake operatives on a specific mission: to take what Winston had sold to China."

"Surely the Orel i Zmeya tag team's Silver Bullet trailer gave us some clues," I declare.

"Luckily, yes." Ryan picks up a phone. Next thing we know, he's barking, "Dominic! Quit flirting with my assistant and get in here—*pronto!*"

While the rest of us flinch, our debonair British

colleague takes his sweet time. Even before he saunters in and drops onto an empty chair, Ryan is seething.

After our boss collects himself, he clicks on one of the wall-sized monitors. A montage of the deadly duo appears. The photos always have the camper in the background, but the photos' points-of-view always include a panorama of some incredibly tasty sky candy: the Grand Canyon; the Grand Tetons: palm trees on a snow-white beach along a turquoise shore; and the Pacific Ocean from a Big Sur cliff. "As it turns out, their names are Randy and Candy Murphy," Ryan explains. "They are—that is, they were—one of the top influencer accounts on the social media website, FaceStaTweet."

"Okay, I'll bite," Jack says. "What exactly is an 'influencer'?"

"Someone who posts so often and so appealingly that they attract a very large following," explains Emma.

"Like, in the mid-eight figures," Arnie chimes in. "And they make a ton of dough doing it. A mega-influencer can make millions of dollars!"

"Then I assume every actor, musician, and athlete has an account," Jack replies.

Arnie snickers. "Yeah...on practically every platform! TikTok, Twitter, Facebook, Instagram, Pinterest, FaceStaTweet, you name it!"

"With forty thousand-plus followers, the Murphys were in a category called macro-influencers, which is a step below mega status," Ryan explains. "Their category includes a lot of B-level celebs, but also people who have a certain expertise that makes their posts—some stills, but usually videos—catnip to subscribers who aspire to their lifestyle."

"The Murphys' followers are growing at an astronomical rate—so fast, in fact, that it raises a couple of red flags." Emma reveals. "Sure, they're cute, but we're betting that at least one of their followers was the head honcho of Eagle and Snake. He would have reached out via a direct message because private texting on FaceStaTweet is done with what's called a 'secret text app,' similar to what we use here at Acme. The protocol for the app operates in the most constrained environment possible: no usernames, passwords, pins, or logins. It never accesses other outside communications. Instead, it uses end-to-end encryption protocol. No message is stored in your device's data."

"We've hacked the account and taken it over. By altering their uploaded posts and the videos, we can keep the charade going for a while anyway," Ryan adds. "Eventually, Eagle and Snake will reach out to demand an update on their mission. If someone does, we're going to raise the ante on the retrieval fee. I'm sure that will make the contact angry. We'll see how far we can take it before we arrange a drop, then see who shows up."

"Did they send or receive direct messages from anyone else?" Abu asks.

"We wish! But sadly, nope. I guess it was an Eagle and Snake no-no." Emma explains. "Apparently, this is how Eagle and Snake communicates with their soldiers of fortune—at the very least, those who propagate misinformation. It embeds encryptions everywhere: in how they phrase the words in their posts as well as in the photos and videos."

"At the same time, Eagle and Snake uses FaceSta-Tweet's untraceable and erasable direct messaging to send mission directives to their assassins," Ryan adds.

"Our only hope is that by vetting their followers and cross-referencing those of other influencers, we'll pull together a list of viable suspects," Emma explains. "ComInt will analyze the comments for a possible code. From that, we can create a cipher. But it's a long and arduous task. What makes it even harder is that a lot of the Murphys's followers hail from farms."

Dominic's face goes even blanker than it normally is if that's possible. "Is that your way of saying that city dwellers aren't into social media? I beg to differ! In fact, every model I date—none of them are milk maids, I guarantee you—posts constantly on TikTok, Instagram and FaceStaTweet."

Emma rolls her eyes. "As a point of reference, it means that their numbers may have been artificially inflated by fake accounts. It's a service that can be purchased. Usually the SM sites look down their noses at this, but they don't necessarily forbid it."

"Why not?" Jack asks.

Abu guffaws. "It's all in the math. The more followers you have, the more successful the SM site looks to its other subscribers. And as far as the influencers are concerned, having more followers translates into more money that sponsors will pay you. A mega-influencer can make over a million dollars *per post*—and they have their choice of whom they want as sponsors."

"Sign me up," I murmur.

"I'm glad you feel that way because Acme has already done that," Ryan replies.

I gawk at him. "Wait!... I was just joking!"

"I wasn't. Everyone in this room will soon be a FaceSta-Tweet influencer, for a very important reason." As Ryan takes a breath, the whole table leans in his direction.

"If we know this is happening, why can't the FBI just round up the Eagle and Snake operatives who are here stateside?" I ask.

"For one reason, finding one is akin to looking for a needle in a haystack," Ryan explains. "There are almost a billion and a half FaceStaTweet members. Of these, several thousand are mega-influencers. Up until you took down the Murphys, we've had no idea this was Eagle and Snake's communications medium."

"Well, at least that's one good thing that came out of the Granny Doo mission," I declare.

"The FaceStaTweet factor makes it an even bigger dilemma. At least ten major venture capital firms are invested in the company. No need to decimate some of our country's largest financial investors just because they don't know they're betting on the wrong horse."

This voice comes from the door: Mario Martinez is standing there.

"Just in time." Ryan waves him in. "Mario will be our liaison with DNI Branham."

Mario nods to everyone before taking the chair between Jack and me.

"I guess that's reason enough for Branham to keep this mission off the books. That way, when we bring the house down on Eagle and Snake, its American investors won't have legal culpability." Jack's tone reinforces his flippant statement.

"At least they'll have a fat legal loss to write off," I add.

"Such investments keep our economy afloat," Mario counters.

"No, it gives them yet another excuse to avoid paying their fair share of taxes. Maybe that's why some of these very same firms fill the coffers of politicians who refuse to strengthen our corporate tax laws," Jack retorts.

"Stay on task, Craigs." Ryan's tone warns us to keep our lips zipped.

After a moment of silence satisfies him that we're duly chastised, he adds: "We don't yet know how, or what, but we do know when the incident will take place: on Chesapeake Bay."

Jack frowns. "Come again?"

"That's the name of FaceStaTweet's annual awards ceremony," Emma explains. "Sponsors line up to woo influencers. Fans vie for tickets. FaceStaTweet's investors are courted. It's a real love fest."

"It takes place at the end of next week," Ryan adds. He clicks the monitor again.

This time we're looking at a video ad for a humongous state of the art ocean liner. It was taken from a drone that does a slow float-over, then pulls back to get a shot of the Washington D.C. skyline just before the setting sun dips into the western horizon.

"The top five influencers in four categories are treated to an all-expenses-paid weekend on the latest, greatest luxury cruise liner—the Prince Charles," Emma explains.

Dominic gives a low whistle. "Luxe indeed! Sumptuous

suites for three hundred passengers! An elegant ballroom with a tiptop orchestra. Only the best food and wine. Not to mention a world class spa. The masseuses have magical fingers..." he sighs ecstatically. "Especially when plying their trade in one of the many cabanas beside the ship's Olympic-sized pool."

"Once Arnie hacks FaceStaTweet's site and jiggers the numbers so that you are mega-influencers, you'll join the other finalists," Ryan explains.

"I am *so* in!" Abu and Arnie declare in unison. They turn to give each other high-fives.

"We'll certainly need all hands on deck. The place should be crawling with Eagle and Snake operatives and recruiters," Mario reminds us. "Branham believes their fearless leader will finally show him- or herself, and we can cut the organization off at its head."

Dominic shrugs. "Apparently, I'm already a bit of a sensation on FaceStaTweet."

Ryan frowns. "You have an account?"

"But of course! What international man of mystery *doesn't* have one?"

Jack raises his hand. "A *real* one. Or at least one who works at a covert ops organization that forbids it in his employment contract."

With a flick of his wrist, Dominic dismisses his jibe. "Pshaw! It is an imperative if I'm to maintain my cover as a wealthy bon vivant and fashion icon."

I snicker. "Just because you troll models on fashion runways doesn't make you one."

"Tell that to my legion of followers—over ten thousand"—he looks down on his cell's screen—"and counting.

Frankly, it beats any dating app. In fact, it's where I found the sisters I'm seeing now—triplets! Nina, Pinta, and Maria. Perhaps you've heard of them, as they're minor celebs in their own right: the Cannoli Sisters? It was Nina's idea …or perhaps Pinta's?–who can tell them apart?—that I get an account so that they can tag me on our madcap escapades." He opens the app:

Yep, it's a FaceStaTweet account alright. In the video, Dominic lays on a bed with three naked women who slither over him then disappear under his red satin sheets. Soon, only their hands are visible as they undress him.

The camera moves in tight on his ecstatic expression.

Brows rise all around the conference table, but I'm the first to ask: "Are we looking at porn?"

Dominic's throaty chuckles fill the room. "Heavens, no! FaceStaTweet reels are posted *for free*. Ergo, no revenue is being made."

Abu whips out his cell, clicks the app, then swipes until he finds Dominic's account. Gawking as he scrolls through Dominic's feed, he murmurs, "I've got news for you. Just because you weren't paid for it doesn't mean it isn't pornographic."

Arnie slides over so that he can see it too. His eyes open wide. "Um…I can think of at least three countries where you'd be thrown in jail for that!"

I poke Dominic. "Since you know the Prince Charles so well, you can give the rest of us the grand tour."

Dominic straightens up. "I'm sure I'll be too busy signing my fans' autographs, among other things."

Ryan is close enough to snatch Abu's phone out of his hand. After taking a long stare, he tosses it back with a sigh. "You'll be busy, alright, Dominic. If this mission is a success, everyone must pull their weight. Keep the account. Drop the Cannolis. And by the way, from now on, ComInt will do all posting on Acme agents' accounts—"

Dismayed, Dominic slumps in his seat.

Another photo appears on the monitor: "Of which there will be three others," Ryan continues. "Donna, yours is for posting food porn." He winces at the term, but continues: "On it, you'll be known as Miss Delish."

I grin. "Will I be demonstrating my own recipes?"

Ryan thinks for a moment. "Yes, if you want. If need be, we can supplement them with whatever the social media producer feels is needed. She's here now, in the lobby. Her name is Jody Keleske. She'll be styling you for the camera as well as staging content for all the accounts. ComInt will take the text, photos, and videos she creates and regurgitate it into various posts and reels. That way, it will seem that you're continually posting during the event when really you're there doing what you should to accomplish our mission. When it's your turn to work with Jody, you'll be called down to Acme's Lab Room C or its auditorium, whichever is appropriate."

"Ah, yes! I saw her when I came in: the lithe, leggy blonde with the camera. I'll be sure to show her my wide-angle lens." Dominic smiles, tantalized at the thought.

"Do me a favor and keep your 'lens' under wraps. She won't have time for your shenanigans," Ryan warns him. "Abu, your cover is as a beatboxer."

Abu grimaces. "I can groove, no problem. But I don't know how to amplify."

"We've got you covered," Emma replies. "We've

invited the best beatboxer in the world—Mark Martin—to train you so that you can mimic him. He'll then dub the vocals for you."

Satisfied, Abu nods. "Great! I'm going to call myself 'The Sleek Sikh.' Catchy, right?"

Arnie nods enthusiastically. "And me, boss?" he asks hopefully. "Do I finally come out into the light?"

"Yeah, okay." Ryan sighs. "With what I've seen of Face-StaTweet influencers, I figure it's the one place where you won't stand out like a sore thumb. Your category is 'game streamer,' whatever that means."

"Oh my God! It's my dream job!" Arnie leaps up and kisses Ryan.

I've never seen our boss's face quite like it looks now: a frozen mixture of shock, horror, and bewilderment—

Until it defrosts into barely tethered fury. Finally, Ryan hisses: "If you ever do that again, you'll get your wish—*if I don't kill you first.*"

Arnie is smart enough to skedaddle—to the other end of the conference table.

"Can someone tell the rest of us what just happened here?" I ask.

"Digital gaming has become one of the driving forces of internet eCommerce," Emma explains. "Not only do gamers interact with each other online, they also watch the big scorers play, sometimes hours on end. The game companies and game developers have created their own private platforms and have also embraced cloud gaming, which is a way that players can tap into games-on-demand, like when you stream a movie. The game *Tower of*

Power is offered exclusively on FaceStaTweet, so it puts all its gaming promotional efforts there."

"What does any of this mean for Arnie?" Jack asks.

Emma rolls her eyes. "Since it's his favorite game in the whole world, essentially, it means he won't be sleeping—or doing much else with either me or Nicky, since gamers with big followings must play continually to keep their scores high and their viewers happy."

"I'm calling my account 'Locked and Loaded with Arnie.'" Our overjoyed tech op snaps his fingers: "Hey, I've got a great idea! Since the camera on the gamers shoots them from behind or from the side, I'll create a deepfake of myself while playing. I'll even lock and load an audio library of every gaming term I'd use, as well as my typical verbal chatter. That way, ComInt can create and upload new dialogue every day."

Emma groans. "In other words, a lot of curse words. Make sure you complete this project here at the office so that Nicky doesn't learn any new gems."

Arnie and Emma's four-year-old already has quite the potty mouth on him. Frankly, I think that's more Emma's fault than Arnie's.

"Brilliant," Ryan exclaims.

Redeemed from our boss's wrath, Arnie practically glows until Ryan adds, "A word to you, and everyone else: don't let your newfound celebrity status go to your head. *This is a mission.* And this time, no friendly operatives are going to die on our watch."

Arnie's smile fades. He gets it. Field work is dangerous.

"So then, what's my cover?" Jack asks.

"FaceStaTweet is wooing Acme Industries for an investment in its growing platform," Ryan explains. "Your title is Vice President of New Ventures. As such, you're in the VIP section with the rest of the money men and women—which is where I'm sure you'll also find the head of Eagle and Snake. Count heads and figure out where the bodies are buried. Hopefully, none will be our own." He turns off the monitor. "Now, in this order, you're to head over to Acme costume and makeup and then meet with Jody. First Arnie, then Dominic. Donna, my guess is that you'll need more time in costume and makeup, so you'll be in the third slot. Abu, Mark is waiting in Acme's auditorium where he'll train you in some beatboxing fundamentals. Donna will come get you when she's done. While Jody is filming you, ComInt is creating your fake FaceStaTweet accounts and seeding them with stills." He stands up. "Party's over, people. Get moving."

As we file out the door, Ryan adds: "Mario and Jack, join me in my office, please."

"You're a natural at this," Jody tells me.

She's talking about the ease I have on camera as I talk through the directions for creating the perfect way to make seven-minute egg-white icing for cakes. In post-production, Jody will add cute upbeat background theme music.

We've completed five videos, each showcasing a different cooking tip: one on how to make the perfect poached egg; another on quick but tasty scalloped potatoes, a third on baking a crisp, juicy chicken; and then one on how to make an easy pot pie with the leftovers. For the most part, though, she has me introducing recipe names and some closing sentences. The rest of the finished posts will be closeups of her hands mixing ingredients or holding the finished dish with my prerecorded voiceover.

Yesterday, Lab Room C was a morgue. Overnight, Acme's cleaners transformed it into a fully-stocked kitchen with pots, pans, a portable pantry—and even a Viking range. I guess Ryan figured its shiny white walls and stainless-steel countertops would look the part and come in handy, as does the refrigerator that once held a few body parts. Talk about quick work!

So that most video mistakes can be fixed in post-editing, Jody has placed several cameras around the counter, all of which are shooting me at different angles. While filming each recipe, she'll create numerous videos as well as some still shots.

To be honest, I feel silly demonstrating my culinary skills in the outfit she's chosen for me. Miss Delish is supposed to be a totally retro homemaker, a throwback to the nineteen-fifties ideal of the perfect little wifey.

As if. Seriously—says who?

To create this persona, Jody scored a waist-cinching thigh-hugging Dior gown and pearls which I wear with an auburn wig teased up into a bouffant. To top off this posh and prissy look, I wear elbow-length white gloves and have a beauty mark on the right side of my lips, ala Marilyn Monroe.

"If my voice comes out breathless, it's because I can barely breathe, let alone speak," I grumble.

"That's quite alright," Jody insists. "In fact, if you can

fake a Southern accent, all the better. It'll go nicely with your cover."

I laugh at the suggestion. "I'll just copy yours."

"Ha! Don't do too good a job of it unless you want that lounge lizard, Dominic, panting after you. Talk about a guy who's full of himself!" Jody rolls her eyes. "Not to mention a big flirt. Is he like that with every woman?"

"Sadly, yes." I put down the spatula that I've been using to swirl the icing onto a chocolate layer cake. "But I've known him long enough to figure out it's all bluster. Beneath that glossy exterior is a kind and overly sensitive guy." After a pause, I add: "He's been…hurt."

Jody's scowl softens. "If you say so. I guess I've just been around too many humongous egos. Social Media is full of them. I've forgotten how to recognize a beautiful soul, especially when it's disguised as a lascivious prig." She chuckles. "At least these shoots pay better than dealing with bridezillas. I used to be a wedding photographer."

"Trust me, if you put Dominic in his place, he'll back off on the playboy antics." I look at my watch. "How many more videos do you need from me?"

"Just one more," Jody assures me. "Have you got a simple three-ingredient recipe that we can shoot in under five minutes?"

I'm just about to answer her when my cell rings:

Mary. She wouldn't be calling unless it's urgent.

"What's up, honey?" I ask.

She's not talking. *She's sobbing*—loudly and incoherently. I can barely make out her words: something about a suspension for using her phone during class to send a text filled with obscenities.

"Mary, dear, I can barely make out what you're saying!"

Finally, she hisses, "Mom, just...come now to school! Vice Principal Vernon wants to see us...together."

"Dad and I are on our way!"

"No! Please...not Dad," she begs.

"But...he'll want to be there for you! He's in a meeting now, with Ryan and Mario—"

"Oh my God! *Mario is in Hilldale too?* Please, you mustn't say anything to him! I'll lose my internship! I'll lose...everything!" She's breathing so heavily now that I know she's hyperventilating. "Please Mom! Just you!"

"Okay, okay...I...I promise." Clicking off, I wave to Jody. "So sorry! An emergency at home. Shall I send in Abu?"

Jody nods. "You're so lucky to have children. "It was always my goal, but... Well, I never met my Prince Charming." She shakes her head. "Too many empty tuxes, if you know what I mean."

"I do."

Yes, I know I'm lucky. But every action comes with a price. This is true even for our children.

In Mary's case, I hope the consequence won't cost her dearly.

Crisis Management

INEVITABLY, SOMEONE IN YOUR FAMILY WILL HAVE A SOCIAL *media crisis. By that, I mean something that damages your family's brand.*

As to what constitutes its "brand?" Easy answer: think of it as those humble-bragging tidbits you put in those year-end letters to every friend and relative about how happy, healthy, serene, and successful you and your family have been over the previous twelve months.

Leaving out the fact that your youngest was just released from juvie may be fudging the truth of your family fantasy, but hey, nobody likes bad news, right?

So, guess who gets to handle it? Why, you, of course.

Here's what constitutes a crisis:

Example 1: Your husband posts something akin to putting his virtual foot in his mouth, causing a shite-storm in the Twittersphere.

Crisis management solution: Delete his account. If need be, put him in Witness Protection too.

Example 2: Your toddler recorded you bad-mouthing your in-laws, then accidentally sent it to them as a text.

Crisis management solution: Take the phone away from the little genius. Then you and your husband both go into Witness Protection. Just make sure the kids aren't left in the custody of your in-laws.

Example 3: you get a call from your teen's school informing you of something cruel or lascivious that your child wrote in a text or created as a video that was then forwarded to classmates.

Crisis management solution: Incinerate all family cell phones. Then the whole lot of you go into Witness Protection.

Notice a pattern here? Let me make it simple for you:

No phones. No accounts,

No brand management needed.

That fantastical year-end letter will do nicely.

I MAKE IT TO HILLDALE HIGH SCHOOL IN RECORD TIME. I'LL be honest, though: I'm not proud of the fact that I ditched the motorcycle cop on the Four-O-Five who stopped me for a ticket just because I drove on the shoulder to get around a stalled truck.

And, no matter what the officer driving the Black-and-White who picked up my tail from there says, it was him, not me, who caused the four-car fender-bender at the One-Ten turnoff. Can I help it if he couldn't follow my car-ski defensive driving maneuver on the Two-Thirteen turnoff?

And it certainly wasn't my fault those four cars happened to be Code Threes (lights-and-sirens) who were also giving chase. Seriously, don't cops still take defensive driving courses?

One must practice what one preaches.

I swerve toward the front entrance, screech to a stop, and head inside.

The hall monitor, who wants to give me a demerit for running into the reception area, changes his mind when he can't catch up with me. Winded, he collapses against a wall of lockers.

No one runs faster than a mother when her child needs her.

MARY IS SEATED IN THE RECEPTION OFFICE. SHE STARES straight ahead. When she hears my footsteps, she turns toward me. Her face is tearstained.

I drop into the chair beside her. Then I take her hand and squeeze it.

The school receptionist nods at me before buzzing Vice Principal Vernon to let him know I'm here. Mary and I sit silently until he opens the door.

He's not smiling.

Noting this, Mary's back stiffens. But as we rise and walk in, Mary holds her head high.

VERNON IS A TALL MAN WITH A SHAGGY MANE OF GRAY HAIR. His suit is rumpled, and his tie askew. The dark skin under his eyes is evidence of his lack of sleep.

I have two teens and a tween. I can't even imagine supervising five hundred of them for eight hours a day for one hundred and eighty days out of the year.

Although I hold out my hand, he ignores it. Instead, he ushers us to join him around the small conference table.

Before he sits down, he takes a laptop off his desk and places it in front of himself. "Thank you for joining us, Mrs. Craig." He looks at me, and pays no attention to Mary.

"Of course. Now, please tell me, Mr. Vernon. What is it exactly that Mary is supposed to have done?"

"We had a complaint from a few parents—their children are also seniors—of a particular video that made the rounds last night among members of Mary's class via one of the social media platforms. It shows Mary in... well, in an unfavorable light."

"In what way?"

"From what I can see... It seems that she is...well, she's having sex—"

"What!" I turn to Mary.

She shakes her head adamantly. "Mom, I swear—*it's not me!*"

He sighs. "The school is quite aware that some of our students are sexually active with or without their parents' approval. However, the fact that she is doing so with several male students, concurrently, and that the video was made here on campus before it was uploaded onto the social media platform that a lot of the students use these days called SnapCrap—"

Nodding, I lay my hand over Mary's. "Vice Principal Vernon, may I see it?"

Hesitantly, he opens the laptop. With a click, the sound of sensual moaning begins, but Vernon is quick to turn the laptop in my direction.

The video starts with a closeup of Mary's ecstatic face before moving over her naked body. A male head is below her waist. The act seems to take place on a bench in a locker room. Throughout the video, Mary's groans turn to purrs and cajoles. The young man moves up—

But then a male voice says, "Hey, share and share alike, right?"

Mary laughs. "I've got a better idea, boys. How about we—"

I close the computer's lid so that I can't hear what she's proposing. To get the image of what I've seen out of my brain, I close my eyes.

"That is not any part of me!" Mary grabs my arm and squeezes it until I open them again. Watching me intently, she adds, "Not my body. Not me speaking. Mom, you must believe me!"

Mutely I nod. Then I turn to Vernon. "I believe my child."

He leans back in his chair. Smirking, he retorts, "You parents! Even with concrete evidence, you always take your child's side!"

"Everything about this could have been simulated—Mary's voice, that...that body..."

But then, who else knows about the mole on the left side of Mary's belly button?

When I pause, Mary's eyes widen.

She knows that I now doubt her.

The tears roll harder and faster down her cheeks.

"Her suspension starts immediately." Vernon's tone is frigid. "And the privilege of being class valedictorian has been withdrawn."

"I believe my daughter," I insist. "If we're able to prove that Mary was set up, will you reinstate her in class, and as valedictorian?"

He considers this. "How would you do so?"

"Through tech forensics, we may be able to assess the account to which the video was uploaded as well as how it was created and altered."

"What you're saying is that you feel what we see may have been computer-generated? Her body, her face, her voice—everything?" By his tone I know he's not convinced.

"Yes, that is exactly what I'm saying. It's done all the time, and for this specific purpose—to ruin reputations."

Vernon sighs. He stares at Mary. "You're lucky to have a mother who believes in you so greatly that she's willing to prove beyond a shadow of a doubt that someone has set you up."

"So, that's a yes?" Mary asks.

He nods. "If Mrs. Craig is correct, the perpetrator will be prosecuted. I'm sure there are laws that cover this kind of...theft." He stands up. "Graduation is a week from this Friday. You have until then to prove your innocence —*beyond a shadow of a doubt.*"

One way or another, someone will pay for this.

And it will not be Mary.

～

"So, who do you think did this to you?" I ask.

I park the car a few doors down from our house. Up until now, the ride home has been made in silence.

"I've been asking myself the same question," Mary admits. "I don't know who would be so cruel. It came to Babs anonymously. She texted the link to me immediately. A moment later, Wendy did the same thing." Her eyes glaze with tears. "But by then practically the whole world had seen it."

"Maybe the culprit is a boy you'd rejected," I suggest.

"Everyone knows that Evan and I have been exclusive for a couple of years now…" Mary pauses in thought. "Last month, a boy in my home room, Lucas Tatum, asked me out. When I told him I was seeing someone, he thought I was brushing him off. Now whenever I say hello, he shrugs and turns away. One of his buddies told me he thinks I'm a…" Mary blushes. "Well… a prick-tease."

Yikes. "Perhaps this guy just can't take no for an answer, and this is his payback," I reply.

"He hears it often enough." Mary shrugs. "He gets rejected a lot."

"He's certainly a suspect then."

"How exactly will we be able to determine if he had anything to do with it?"

"What he did to you was breaking the law," I remind her. "If you suspect him, we'll get a search warrant."

"But what if he didn't do it? We'll have made our suspicions public, and he'll feel awful and…ashamed!" Mary's lips tremble at the thought.

"Just like whoever did this to you made you feel ashamed—and is trying to ruin your reputation."

My daughter slumps down in her seat. "All the more reason I'd hate to do the same to someone else, especially if they had nothing to do with it! We will have violated his privacy!"

I pat Mary's hand. "I understand. First things first. We start by hacking the site where it was uploaded."

"But… isn't that illegal?" Mary asks.

I'm about to answer when a car drives by: it belongs to the other mother in my carpool: Penelope Bing.

Jeff and his friend, Morton, are in the backseat. Cheever, Penelope's son, sits in the front passenger seat.

By now, news of the video with Mary's double will have been all over school.

I'm just about to suggest that we duck, but I'm too late. Cheever sees us. It's all too obvious when he shoves his fist against his mouth a few times in tandem with using his tongue to pop out his cheek, as if simulating a blow job.

Mary scowls. "I want to smack that smirk off his ugly mug!"

I stymie the urge to say *you have my permission*. Instead, I declare, "Just ignore him. Head on into the house and don't look back."

To my dismay, Penelope stops her car in front of my driveway, blocking it.

I toot my horn. When she glances back, she does a doubletake. I motion her to move up. She does so—but also shuts off the engine and opens her door to get out.

As quick as he can, Jeff leaps out of the car, too.

Only then do I notice that Mario's car is in our driveway, behind Aunt Phyllis's ancient Volkswagen Beetle, which is tucked in our garage. She's already picked up Trisha from school. I take it that Mario gave Jack a lift home.

Or perhaps he's here to see Mary.

Mary must be thinking the same thing because when she notices Mario's car, all the color goes out of her face. Still, she opens her door and gets out.

Penelope calls out Mary's name, but she ignores her.

Good girl.

When Jeff reaches his sister's side, he takes her hand. They walk in together.

"HOW RUDE OF YOUR DAUGHTER TO IGNORE ME!" PENELOPE huffs. "Well, I guess I should have expected it."

"Why, how perceptive of you to realize that my daughter has had an awful day," I purr.

"I am nothing of the sort," Penelope retorts.

No shit. "It was meant as a joke," I declare.

"Well, then, I guess the last laugh is on her—and you, for allowing your daughter to defile herself! And so publicly, at that!" she scolds back.

"That was not Mary. Someone doctored that video."

Penelope's eyes narrow. "A deadbeat parent will do anything—even doubt their own eyes—to ignore the obvious."

I sneer, "It takes one to know one."

"How dare you!" Penelope's rage has her shaking.

"Cheever is everything that makes a mother proud: kind, successful, popular—"

I guffaw. "Wait… We're still talking about your kid, right? The one who makes lousy grades, has worse manners than a hog, is rude, crude, and a total goon?" I point to Cheever.

Unaware that he's being watched, he picks his nose.

Haughtily, Penelope hisses, "I'll have you know that my son made over a hundred thousand dollars this year! Not bad for a high school sophomore."

"What did he do, rob a bank?"

"That's a dirty rumor!" Penelope sputters. "Can he help it if he looks like the robber's mug shot in the post office?" Proudly she adds, "I'll have you know that he's the most watched live-stream player on his favorite gamer platform. He gets close to three hundred chatbox messages each minute! In fact, the platform has given him a coveted ten-hour time slot! It's called 'Leave it to Cheever.' Three major sponsors have already signed up. They want to tap into his millions of fans who love his rants."

He's learned at the feet of a master. Penelope is barely coherent on a good day. Right now, best as I can tell she's speaking gibberish.

I shrug. "Just goes to show how many folks need to get off the Internet and get a real life."

Frankly, I can barely stomach a fifteen-minute car ride with the kid, what with all the non-stop crap he spews.

Out of the corner of my eye, someone is waving to me from the living room window: it's Jack. "Now if you'll excuse me, I've got places to go and people to see."

"Wait, Donna… You see, the reason I feel we need to

talk is that Cheever and I want to lend our support to Mary."

Penelope has got something up her sleeve…

"Do tell," I murmur.

"Before Mary's reputation is in total tatters, Cheever feels she should have an opportunity to give her side of the story."

"Oh… Well, we've already talked with Vice Principal Vernon. If Cheever is suggesting that she speak at the next all-school assembly, that may not be such a bad idea—"

"He's got something even better in mind!" Eagerly, she leans into the window. "He's offering to devote a full hour interview to her on 'Leave it to Cheever.' Imagine what she could do with that forum at her fingertips!"

"Not on your life," I snap.

"At least think about it," she implores.

Instead, I rev my engine.

Penelope takes the hint and leaps back out of my way as I screech into my garage.

I don't know how many people saw the fake video on SnapCrap. Even if Penelope isn't blowing smoke about Cheever's millions of followers, the last thing I need them to do is turn their attention on Mary.

That video was not the sort of undercover position she'd hope for.

Mary is sitting with Jack and Mario in our formal living room. I nod to them, then position myself so that I can look in the media room.

Through its large picture window, I see that Jeff is outside with Trisha and Aunt Phyllis. As my aunt shouts out encouragement, Jeff and Trisha go through a few soccer passing drills. I'm glad that Jeff is off Trisha's case about her cooking. My kids know when it's time to circle the wagons. Someone's got a target on Mary's back. When we discover who, I'm sure that, like me, Jeff will want to hang the culprit from the nearest tree.

As I'd suspected, Jack and Mario are questioning Mary about her knowledge of the incident. After she repeats when and how she found out about the video, she mentions Lucas as a possible suspect.

"How old are you?" Mario asks.

"Seventeen…for another few days," Mary answers. She looks only at Jack. She's too ashamed to face Mario. "By the way, Mom, you can cancel the surprise birthday party you had planned. At this point, none of my so-called friends want to be anywhere near me, let alone at some bash in my honor."

I flinch at the pain in Mary's voice—and at the news that my secret wasn't one at all.

"The reason I ask is that, in California, eighteen is the age of consent," Mario explains. "Were the person in the video actually you, it would be statutory rape, and the men perpetrating the act would be charged for it."

"But…since that isn't really me, will the charge stand up in court?" Mary wonders.

"In this case, the video was digitally altered to make it look like you. Such videos are known as 'deepfakes,' and are illegal in California and Texas, but not yet in every state. To take it one step further, in our country this specific sort of deepfake— non-consensual pornography known as a 'deepnude'—is clearly viewed as a sex crime. As such, the producer and distributor would also face a criminal charge. Ironically, ninety-six percent of all deepfakes are deepnudes. The majority of those are perpetrated against women—usually actors or pop singers—or as in your case, non-celebrity women as revenge porn."

"That's just great! I get to experience the downside of celebrity without being one." Mary harrumphs. "So, what exactly happens if we take out a warrant on Lucas?"

"Either local law enforcement or the FBI may confiscate any and all devices," Mario replies.

"But I don't know for sure that Lucas had anything to do with it," Mary insists. "I'd hate for him to be put in an embarrassing situation before we know one way or another."

I add, "I was about to explain to Mary how we could expose the culprit, but then Penelope sidelined me."

Hearing our neighbor's name, Jack groans. "What did *she* want?"

I shrug. "Some silliness. I told her to leave us alone." No need to add that I'll make her life miserable if she ignores my warning. Jack can hear it in the tone of my voice. "Mario, under what conditions could a warrantless search be granted?" I ask.

"We'll have the go-ahead to hack his phone and his computer," he replies.

"But… that's not legal, is it?" Mary asks. "Doesn't that violate his Fourth Amendment rights?"

"If there's probable cause to believe that this Lucas kid sent any sort of media electronically that contained any evidence of a crime, or if it was instrumental in perpetrating one, then yes, we'd have reason to deploy NIT malware without a search warrant," Mario explains.

"What does NIT stand for?" Mary asks.

"Network Investigative Technique," Mario explains.

I nod to Mary. "In other words, Lucas will never know we went looking for the smoking gun in his devices."

She wavers, but only a moment. "Please then, let's apply for it."

Jack asks, "How soon will it take to get the approval on the NIT?"

"Give me seventy-six hours," Mario replies.

"I can't just twiddle my thumbs during that time, wondering if I'll ever get my name cleared. Mario, if you need me to start my internship early, I'm up for it," Mary says.

"After the warrant is issued and we know more, we'll take it from there," Mario replies. "In the meantime, I'm sure Acme could use your knowledge of social media to assist in the preparation of their next mission."

Mary shifts her gaze to me. "What do you think about that?"

"Well, considering you practically live on Instagram, TikTok, and FaceStaTweet, I'm sure you know a trick or two that might be helpful."

Mary gives me a thumbs up before heading outside to be with Aunt Phyllis, Jeff, and Trisha.

Mario looks down at his watch. "I should pull out. I've got a conference call with DNI Branham in an hour."

Jack and I follow him to the door. "Mario, when the NIT comes through, would you mind tossing that project to Acme?" Jack asks. "Something tells me Mary would prefer us to handle the hack and analysis. You know, keep it in the family."

Mario thinks for a moment. "That's doable. All I ask is that you dot all your I's and cross all your T's."

"Don't we always?" Jack and I say in unison.

Mario laughs so hard that he's still doubled over as he gets into his car.

From what we can see, he doesn't stop laughing until his car is halfway down the block.

As Jack turns to join the others, I ask, "So, what was the powwow with Branham all about?"

He grimaces. "Sorry, can't say, Donna."

"But... it's about the mission, right? So why keep me in the dark?"

Jack shrugs. "You know the rules: each of us is informed on a need-to-know basis."

Grrrrr.

Still, I smile.

I know I've got some Sodium Pentothal left over from a previous mission. Cocktail hour should be interesting.

5

Clickbait

Any sort of video, photo, or text that encourages users to click onto it is known as "clickbait."

A lounge chair on a white sandy beach beside a turquoise ocean is clickbait.

A well-endowed gal showing decolletage is clickbait.

A cute puppy or adorable kitten is clickbait.

So is any statement that angers you, inspires you, or lures you to hit the button that takes you to the rest of its message.

As with another sort of bait, say, "jailbait," falling to temptation can only lead to trouble.

Solution: avert your eyes and keep your hands to yourself.

"Guess who is the numero uno Acme influencer?" Arnie's robot dance is too close for comfort. Our accounts have only been live for a few days. It's true he's in the lead, but Abu is a close second.

As for me…

Well, let's just say I'm not the media phenom I'd assumed I'd be.

So when Arnie's hand ends up in front of my nose, I swat it away. "Boasting is no way to win friends and influence enemies," I growl.

"Who needs friends when you've got over thirty million followers?"

I slap him on his noggin. "You do remember that this is all make-believe, right? We're trying to stop a terrorist act."

Arnie scowls. "You can be such a downer. It's hard to tell you're even related to Mary."

I grab him by his collar. "What do you mean by that?"

He stutters, "Only that… Well, she's sweet. Easy going. Creative."

I tighten my chokehold. "Oh yeah? Where do you think she gets those wonderful traits, numbskull?"

By now, Arnie is gasping.

Jack taps me on the shoulder. "Um… Don, I think you've made your point. What do you say we take a little breather?"

Arnie wheezes, "Me…too! Must…breathe! … Passing…out…"

I loosen my grip. "You're right, Jack. I could do with some fresh air."

Lightning quick, Arnie scurries away.

Jack puts his arm around me. "Admit it. You're jealous."

"*Of Mary?*" I snort. "Hardly. She's not exactly living la vida loca. Between worrying about her reputation and whether the NIT will be approved, coupled with dealing with Arnie's hairbrained antics for his stupid little videos, no wonder she's so jumpy. Not to mention his B.O. will eventually make her faint—"

"Not Mary. I meant Arnie. You're jealous of his follower numbers."

I shrug. "Maybe… Okay, yeah. How come his numbers are so great while mine suck? And it's not just him, either. Abu is right on his heels. Even Dominic's are better than mine—without the triplets, no less!" Frustrated, I shake my head. "The invitations for the Faceys go out in two more days. If I don't make the cut—"

"If you don't make the cut, you'll figure out a way to work behind the scenes, so quit sweating it," Jack warns. "What are you at now?"

"Only 17 million. I just can't figure it out! Neither can Jody. The recipes are simple. The end results are gorgeously mouthwatering. And I certainly look and sound great on camera—"

"Maybe that's part of the issue," Mary says.

She's standing behind us.

"What do you mean?" I ask.

"Maybe you're doing everything too perfect. Wouldn't it be more natural if you messed up every now and again? I don't know…maybe set a cake on fire or something." She shrugs. "I'm just saying that it may make you more relatable. Julia Child didn't always get it right. From what I understand, her missteps made her more relatable." She giggles. "Listen, don't tell Arnie but I think that the reasons his videos are such a hit isn't because he's one of the top five *Tower of Power* scorers but because his comments are really, really inane. I mean, like, wincingly awful."

I sigh. "Maybe you're right. Leaving a flub or two in may do the trick. I'll talk to Jody about it." I pause, then add: "Perhaps you'd like to sit in on the shoot. That way if you think of something that may work—"

"I'd love that!" Mary looks behind her. Assured that no one can overhear us, she adds, "To be honest, Arnie's idea of 'creativity' is getting down to the level of fart jokes. Let's just say he's no Michael Che."

Jack puts an arm around each of us. "Team Craig. Love it! And if we need another reason for a group hug, here's one: Mario got approval for the NIT."

Mary murmurs, "Then Arnie will be doing the hack on Lucas soon."

"In a couple of hours, in fact. And if he's successful— I'm guessing he can outsmart the firewall in a disaffected teen's computer—we should know if Lucas is indeed the culprit." Jack nods in my direction. "Now, go make your mama an internet star."

"Mary, your idea is brilliant!" Jody exclaims. "Donna, look! The 'Feel the Burn' video has only been up a half-hour and already you've gotten more hits than all the other videos combined. Not to mention you've quadrupled your followers."

It's taken us until mid-afternoon to shoot ten more videos. In doing so, any real-time mishaps were left in the final cut.

In one, I burn my hand while pulling a pan of grilled root vegetables from the oven. We also filmed my first aid for the burn.

And we bleeped my curses.

In another video, I lift the head of the mixer a second before turning it off and get sprayed with cake batter. You can hear Jody and Mary laughing in the background. It was Mary's brilliant idea.

And while flambéing bourbon shrimp, I squealed when the flame flashed far above my comfort zone. "That was a close one," Jody had murmured.

Mary now points out: "As of five minutes ago, you're tied with Abu for followers."

"Thank goodness!" I declare. "Who knew that pretending to be a kitchen klutz would be such a comfort to others?"

"I guess I'll have to break the news to Abu that he's got real competition."

I laugh. "Better you than me."

Jody walks to the door and peeks out— "Oh!... Dominic is early for his session." She smiles. "Our shoots having been taking place in various L.A. hotspots. I thought I knew them all, but he's proven that I've barely scratched the surface."

"If there's one thing Dominic knows is where to see and be seen," I acknowledge. Teasingly, I add, "I hope he's being a gentleman."

"Oh, he is." Jody shrugs. "To be frank, after what I saw of his FaceStaTweet account, I'm surprised." She smiles coyly. "And, admittedly, a bit disappointed."

"Take it as a good sign. It means he's not just plucking your heartstrings for a quick ditty."

Jody laughs. "If you say so." She walks to the door and beckons him in.

Dominic walks in with his hands behind his back. Seeing Mary and me, his face turns bright red. "Oh! I didn't know you were still here."

"Just leaving," I reply as I untie my apron.

"Wow! Two dozen pink roses!" Mary has moved behind Dominic. "Are you going to use them as a prop during the shoot?"

"No! … I mean…" Dominic's stammer trails off. He stares at me. "Shouldn't you be at Trisha's soccer game, or something?"

"In fact I'm headed there now," I retort. I nod to Mary. "Aunt Phyllis will be there too, and so will Jeff. Why don't you ride along with me? It looks like Jody has Dominic covered." I sneak a wink to our producer, who blushes.

When Dominic winces at my double entendre, I realize the seriousness of his intentions.

Well, whattaya know. He's making his move!

Mary frowns, but then says, "Sure, why not. Is Dad coming too?"

"Sadly, no. But he'll be home in time for dinner," I reply. I toss her the car fob.

Mary guffaws. "You're letting me drive?"

"A lot has changed in the past seventy-two hours," I point out, "including your priorities."

"I guess losing your friends, your future—your whole life as you know it—will do that to you." She grabs her backpack. "But sure, let's go. No better way to test my new skill for hiding in plain sight."

THE DRIVE OVER TO HILLDALE ELEMENTARY SCHOOL IS bumper-to-bumper.

"I hope we get there before it's over," I grumble.

Mary hasn't said much. I don't know if she's sweating the warrant approval or the horror of running into some of her school pals. To get her mind off both, I say, "Dad told me you were a great shot on Acme's shooting range."

"Apparently I have a knack for obliterating targets from the center out." Her giggle is uneasy. "But Dad has warned me that killing a person is different. Tomorrow morning, we'll be doing some hand-to-hand combat: taekwondo, boxing, jiujitsu. He been teaching me the basics since ninth grade—Jeff and Trisha too—but I've got to up my game."

"How does all of this defensive training make you feel?"

"Frankly, I feel empowered," Mary assures me. "But if I'm ever in a position of kill or be killed… well, we'll see if I have it in me." She shrugs. "By the way, Dad wants you to do my knife fight training."

After what I did to Randy Murphy in Grammy Doo's Diner, I can see why.

"Tomorrow is Friday. We'll leave work in the early afternoon and start then, if you like."

She nods, satisfied. "Dad also suggested that I should do a survival course this summer, before my internship."

"I agree with him… Hey, I've got a great idea! Why don't we make it a mother-daughter adventure? Middle of nowhere, deep in the woods with no cell phones and a couple of tricked out Swiss Army knives? With those, we have the perfect weapon. I'll also teach you how to make a weapon from just about anything."

"The middle of nowhere sounds perfect. No one calls me anyway." Mary's tone drips with sarcasm. A few moments later, she sighs. "Sorry, Mom. Yeah, okay, I'm all for getting away."

"Are you saying you haven't heard from Wendy or Babs?"

"Babs has sent me a few texts. I'm just not in the mood to answer them."

"Well, I'm glad that she's reached out. You were there for her when she desperately needed a friend." When they were sophomores, a nasty rumor went around about Babs and a junior boy. Mary stood firmly at her side.

"But not Wendy," Mary continues. "I'm sure her mom has insisted that she stay clear of me. She wouldn't want my taint on her precious daughter." Mary shrugs. "That's okay. No better time for a fresh start—especially if Arnie can't root out who ruined my life before Berkeley pulls my admission."

"Arnie works fast," I remind her.

"I hope so. But if he doesn't, at the very least I can forget my troubles by losing myself in my Acme FaceSta-Tweet assignments." She snickers. "I now better understand why you get such a high from working."

"It was how I buried my grief over what I thought was the loss of your biological father," I admit. "But revenge isn't necessarily the healthiest way to channel your pain."

This time, she doesn't respond.

A moment later, we pull into the Hilldale Elementary parking lot. Suddenly, Mary does a doubletake. "My God, that's Evan's car!"

I look to where she's pointing. "Did you tell Evan you'd be here?"

Mary shakes her head. "My guess is that he got ahold of Jeff, who told him we were on our way."

"Haven't you talked to him since the whole video incident?"

Mary shrugs. "He knows about it and reached out to me, but I haven't responded."

"Why not? Are you afraid he may believe it was you?"

"He knows better. But he won't like it if I get booted out of Berkeley before I get there." Mary rolls her eyes. "And he'll hate the fact that my suspension may mean leaving for DC earlier than I'd anticipated. He'd prefer that I work on his project instead."

"What is it, exactly?"

"All I know is that it's another government contract. As with all of them, it's very hush-hush. Although he did let it slip that it has something to do with tracking and analysis of dark web activity."

"Is there a reason Evan's offer doesn't appeal to you?"

Mary stops short. "I love Evan with all my heart. I want to spend the rest of my life with him. But the next few years will test our love. Between his freshman year workload and the businesses he's inherited through his father's trusts—particularly BlackTech, what with all its government dealings—he's already growing, challenging himself in ways he never thought possible." Her chin juts forward. "I don't take his love—or his respect—for granted. But to keep both, I'll also have to take on new challenges. I want to prove that I can stand on my own two feet—without him, or you, or Dad. Otherwise, we'll grow apart. We're not children anymore."

"You're right. You're a fully realized adult." I turn my head so that Mary doesn't see the tears in my eyes. "I'm so proud to be your mother."

She leans over to kiss my cheek. "We better get to the bleachers. We don't want to miss Aunt Phyllis's Get-Down dance. She pulls out all stops."

"I just pray she doesn't pull a muscle," I mutter.

6

Impressions

IF THERE'S ONE PLACE WHERE THE SAYING "NO NEWS IS GOOD news" is wrong, it's the social media universe. There, it doesn't matter what you post, be it things that make you happy, sad, upset, or angry. The views garnered are measured as "impressions," which the social media platform uses to attract paying sponsors, whose ads run beside it.

Not that you'll ever see a dime of it.

Bottom line: a company is making money from it.

Shouldn't it be you cashing in on your anxious plea for attention?

If you think the answer is yes, you're ready for your close-up as a social media influencer!

Yeah. Um…

Good luck with that.

~

Trisha's game is in the middle of the second period. The score is tied at four each.

The bleachers are almost full. Lee is at the end of the farthest one. Evan, who sits beside him, holds Harrison in his lap. Lee's Secret Service detail—three men and a woman, donning golf shirts, khakis, and baseball caps—is trying to make itself as unobtrusive as possible.

One of the men stands beside Lee. His eyes continually scan those who come and go. Aunt Phyllis's squeeze, Porter, sits directly behind Lee. The female agent sits in front of Lee. Another man stands in front of the bleachers. His eyes dart back and forth, taking in all movement.

By now, Lee's Hilldale neighbors have accepted his presence at Janie's games. They nod their hellos and Lee does the same. When our children score, Lee is just as quick to leap up and slap five as the parents around him.

Invariably, if the team wins, he'll treat everyone to ice cream at the local shop if another parent doesn't beat him to that offer.

If the girls win the tournament, Janie will beg to have them over for a sleepover. Lion's Lair boasts eighty-six rooms—with more than enough bedrooms for each of the girls to have their own.

But what would be the fun in that?

Evan smiles uncertainly when he sees us and hands Harrison to Lee before waving us over.

Mary barely nods. Despite the brave speech she just gave me, I imagine she feels she's got no reason to smile.

Evan steps down from the bleachers to help me up. But before he can do the same for Mary, she takes his hand and walks him away from the bleachers.

She knows she can no longer avoid the heart-to-heart talk they so desperately need.

As I take Evan's place beside Lee, Harrison squeals with delight. He crawls into my lap and pats my cheek.

"Lucky boy," Lee murmurs.

I feel my cheeks heat up. "And a good day to you too, Mr. Chiffray. So, the game is a cliffhanger?"

"You betcha," he declares. "And since two of those goals are Trisha's, your Aunt Phyllis has been strutting her stuff."

"How about Janie?"

Lee puffs up with pride. "I'm proud to say the very first goal was hers. This is an important game, too—the last one of the season—unless they win. And then it's a playoff for first place in their region."

"Oh…so, essentially, I've missed the whole season." *Bad, bad, bad mommy…*

"Don't beat yourself up. Not all of us have the luxury of retirement." His sarcasm is directed at himself.

Not that I blame him. Lee stepped down as President of the United States rather than have his now deceased wife, Babette, exposed as a traitor. He finds his stock portfolio less exciting than the day-to-day business of running the most powerful country in the world.

"Evan told me about Mary's situation." He shakes his head, awed. "The laws about deepfakes—and especially deepnudes—should have been passed by now! Yet another thing we can thank our last POTUS, the dearly deceased Bradley Edmonton, for shelving prior to a Congressional vote."

I snicker. "He was only following orders."

Lee knows what I mean. His successor was a Russian asset. Deepfakes—especially those to wreak scandal on U.S. politicians who are Cold War hawks—are a GVR specialty.

Frankly, had it not been for Lee, Acme wouldn't have been able to bring Edmonton down. He acted as the go-between for Marcus and Ryan, who had changed places when Edmonton fired Marcus and hired Ryan as his replacement. He thought this would ensure that Acme was crippled while I was being blackmailed to do Edmonton's dirty work under the threat of Jack being tried for treason and murder.

"I assume Acme will get to the bottom of Mary's problem?" Lee asks.

I nod. "We're waiting for official clearance as we speak."

"Evan is concerned for Mary. He's afraid that Berkeley will renege on her admission acceptance. I told him I'd pull whatever strings I could—"

"That's very kind of you, Lee. But hopefully, this will all be cleared up in the next day. In any regard, Mario Martinez has assured her that her White House internship won't be affected."

"Ah...well, that's good to know."

"You don't sound convinced."

"It's not that," he insists. "I...well, from what Evan said, I was under the impression that she'd be joining his project in Berkeley."

"Interesting. Because according to the conversation I had with Mary on the way over, that may be wishful thinking on his part."

In unison, our heads turn in Mary and Evan's direction.

From the scowl on Evan's face, he doesn't like what he's hearing from Mary.

I give my daughter credit: as she makes her point, she doesn't raise her voice and her hands stay at her side.

Suddenly our side of the bleacher lets loose with a frenzied roar:

Trisha has scored.

A boom box is playing a tune from Beyoncé's latest album. Aunt Phyllis shakes and shimmies then she locks and pops. She moon-walks the full length of the bleachers, then struts off in the other direction.

The crowd goes wild. It seems that every parent's cell phone is recording her.

Ah, heck.

I fight the urge to beg Arnie to hack all phones within a one-mile radius of me and scrub the video before they are uploaded on social media websites.

But then I think, why rain on Aunt Phyllis's parade?

Yep, it's a parade, alright. Every Hilldale Elementary team player is copying Aunt Phyllis's moves.

She's a phenomenon.

I can't take that away from her.

I hear the faint buzz of my phone over the ruckus: The text, from Jack to Mary and me, is short and terse:

Arnie hacked SnapCrap. Meet us at home.

Mary is waving me over.

"Duty calls. Please tell Phyllis and Trisha that we'll meet them back at the house."

"No problem. We gave them a lift, so we'll drop them off there—hopefully after celebrating with an ice cream run."

When I get to the car, instead of tossing me the key fob, Mary says, "Evan is joining us at the house. Why don't you two ride together?"

Evan is as surprised as me at her request.

I don't argue. I'm sure there's a method to her madness.

"Mary says she's been hanging out at Acme during her suspension." Evan's tone is as easy as if we're discussing the weather.

"Yep. It's kept her mind off that hideous deepnude prank. And she's been very helpful. I never thought I'd say this but for once, I'm glad for all the hours she spends on social media."

"I guess we'll know if Arnie was successful in a few minutes." He hesitates. "If not, I offered to take her back to Berkeley with me. My student advisor, Dr. Wallencraft, says that my student team can always use an extra set of hands—and another brain—on our research project."

"What exactly is it?"

"We're creating the ultimate IoT platform."

I chuckle. "You're talking Greek to me."

"It's an application for secure connectivity. You know for things that need sensor management, like for data collection. IoT is used for mobile software applications, in some cases."

I sigh. "You've now switched from Greek to Latin—

neither of which I'm fluent. My bet is that Mary isn't either."

"She doesn't have to be," Evan insists. "But since my firm, BlackTech, is partnering on the development with Berkeley, it may affect both our futures. I thought that alone would get her excited about it." He frowns.

"I take it she isn't?"

He shrugs. "She insists on interning with Mario." He practically spits out our colleague's name. "She finds it more challenging. She actually said that by focusing her studies in a different field, we'll grow closer." He rolls his eyes. "I don't see how that can happen while she's in DC and I'm on the West Coast."

"Are you asking my opinion?"

"Yes, please."

"Then I have to admit I see her point. Evan, she wants to be your partner. If she's in your shadow, she can't be that. Have you considered how her establishing a relationship with Mario could benefit BlackTech?"

"Depends on how far she'll go to have that relationship," Evan mutters.

I sputter, "You're... *jealous—of Mario*?"

"You sound just like her." I turn so that I can look him in the eye. Thank goodness Evan is driving because unlike me, he's able to keep his eyes on the road. "Hell yeah, I am!" His chin juts out. "She's more excited about seeing him than being with me."

"Some women thrive on jealousy. Mary isn't one of them. She prefers trust."

He doesn't answer. He's too ashamed.

As he should be.

In time, he mutters, "I couldn't bear to lose her."

Once I'd overheard a conversation they'd had—an argument, more like it—in which he admitted as much to her, and with good reason. His father's murder was on his mother's hands.

She died in prison before she could give us some intel that would have allowed Acme to take down the Quorum. It would have gone far to redeem her in her son's eyes.

"I know." I reach over to pat his hand. "The tragic loss of your parents…"

He nods. "If it hadn't been for Mary—and the rest of the Craigs…"

"You're part of our family, Evan. But you must believe that Mario's only interest in Mary is in seeing her succeed in the career she says she wishes to explore—strategic intelligence. Mary's endgame is all about you: she wants to make you proud of her."

"If you say so."

"You'll have to trust me on that."

"No. I have to trust her." He nods. "Otherwise, I will lose her."

He gets it.

And just in time since we're pulling into our driveway.

Evan parks behind Mary. She waits until we alight from his car. When she takes his hand, he squeezes hers.

As they walk in together, she smiles back at me.

ARNIE AND JACK ARE AT THE HOUSE, AS ARE EMMA AND ABU.
And so is Mario.

My surprise only puts a cocky grin on his lips.

"You're like a bad penny, Mario, and all that implies," I declare. "Just when we think we're rid of you, here you are again."

"He's here on my behalf." Marcus' gruff voice comes from Jack's cell, which is on speaker mode.

"Mine too," Ryan adds.

Ouch.

For once, everyone else in the room follows the rule that silence is golden.

Finally, Jack nudges Arnie, who gulps before saying, "I can report unequivocally that Lucas Tanner didn't upload the video."

Mary shuts her eyes. When she falls back onto the nearest wall, Evan does the same, taking her hand in his.

While I'm sure my daughter is glad for Tanner that he wasn't involved, her chance to clear her name in time for graduation has just been reduced by forty percent.

The clock is ticking. And between Arnie's dreams of being a social media phenom and finding Mary's tormentor, he'll have his hands full.

Like the rest of us, Mary braces to hear the rest of what Arnie has to say.

"While the issues of who did this to her, how it was done, and why it was done is still unsolved, we do know the server in which it was uploaded. It's based in Reykjavík, Iceland. A hack is possible, but it will take some time."

"Sorry, I couldn't hear you through the static on my line," Branham growls.

"Neither could I because of the wax in my ear," Mario's

tone is serious, but his smirk infers otherwise. Since the server in question is out of the country, we can skirt US hacking laws. Both men are indicating that what Arnie does—and ergo, Acme—will not be acknowledged by our government.

Arnie yells, "What I said was—"

Emma slaps her hand over his mouth. "What he means to say is that we are exploring all options on ways in which to remove it and track down its producer. There is some good news—though not about that." Emma glances over at Mary and mouths, *Sorry.*

My daughter shrugs.

I turn to Mary and Evan. "You may want to step outside now, since what's to be discussed next is of a sensitive nature."

They nod, but their disappointment is obvious in their crestfallen faces. They're caught up in the room's energy.

"Donna, in fact, Evan and Mary have clearance on this mission."

Shocked, I stutter, "I…I beg your pardon?"

"We'll be sourcing out Mary's personal issue to a reliable Dark Web consultant. I think you'll approve. She's known to us as The Mad Hacker."

"Ah! …Well…" How can I argue with the inclusion of someone who has saved my life on at least two occasions, not to mention helped bring Carl down?

"In the meantime, Mary has already been instrumental in securing your cover," Mario points out. "Until the Mad Hacker comes through with proof of her innocence, Ryan agrees that the mission could do with an extra pair of eyes. The fact that she is a young adult gives her great cover in this particular op. She can cozy up to the other influencers, listen in on their gossip, and feed us intel on which of them don't seem legit to their peers."

"And while she's there, Mary can assist Emma and Arnie with communications and tech-op," Ryan announces.

I turn in such a way that I block Mary from seeing my scowl directed at Mario.

Jack sees it, and shifts his eyes toward a wall, but he's not able to stifle a snicker.

So, this was the discussion he had in Ryan's office with Mario.

Traitor.

"Acme ComInt has been working diligently to make sure our mission team's undercover operatives have enough followers to make the final five influencers in their respective FaceStaTweet categories." As Emma pauses, Arnie, Abu, Dominic and I tense up until she declares: "The finalists were verified ten minutes ago. In all cases, it was neck-to-neck, but yes, you're all finalists. ComInt is monitoring your account emails and will respond affirmatively when the invitation is extended, along with travel and accommodations on the latest luxury ocean liner, the Prince Charles, which is currently docked in Chesapeake Bay, outside of DC. Throughout the weekend, it will cruise the bay."

"Now that Emma's team has the contestant list, we've got profiles on our possible suspects. Invited guests—the two hundred and fifty fans who have won the lottery for paid tickets to the awards ceremony—must also be vetted, as well as the FaceStaTweet's financiers and sponsors. Your

Acme lenses will allow Emma's team to do facial scans, which will be matched with records of known soldiers of fortune. But our files aren't complete, so you must always have your guard up."

"As for Evan, marrying the BlackTech project to this mission will be an ideal test to its capabilities," Marcus declares.

"In what way?" Jack asked.

"Evan why don't you explain it?" Marcus suggests.

"There's an expression that has floated around tech in the last couple of years that is trite but true: 'data is the new oil.' Whereas our country leads the world in internet commerce, our military's technological infrastructure is very last century. We've lost too many of its secrets to foreign hackers—specifically, the Chinese. The MSS—China's Ministry of State Security—is making a full-court press for developing Artificial Intelligence."

"And as your latest mission out in the desert proved, the MSS will do anything to steal ours in order to give it a head start," Ryan adds.

"The quickest way to cut us off at the knees is to go after our infrastructure," Branham chimes in. "The Infrastructure Security Agency has already issued a vulnerability alert. We assume their first target will be our power grid since it keeps us safe—both our military, and our commerce. The chatter we've picked up tells us the Faceys may be used as the launch pad for its AI malware."

"How does BlackTech fit in?" I ask.

"BlackTech has developed a filter that works like a bloodhound: if an AI intruder—that is malware—is lurking, it'll sniff it out," Evan replies.

"How affective has it been in lab tests?" Arnie asks.

"It's worked 89.4 percent of the time."

Arnie nods grudgingly. "Pretty decent odds."

"If Evan is to also be at the Faceys, won't he need a cover?" Mary asks.

"He'll be Miss Delish's producer," Mario replies.

Evan gawks at him. "I'm not much of a cook."

"You don't have to be. Just hold the camera and Acme's producer will take care of the finished product."

Emma looks at her watch. "The private jet FaceSta-Tweet has chartered will be wheels up at nine sharp, tomorrow morning. I would imagine everyone will want time to pack before then." She smiles innocently at Dominic. "By the way, Jody will be going as your producer."

"Ah...well, of course." His coyness does little to cover the fact that he's thrilled about it.

"Signing off, folks," Ryan declares.

"Godspeed," Branham adds.

Evan nods at Mary. "I've got my suitcase in the car. Why don't you meet me in the kitchen and bring me up to speed on what I'll need to do to assist your mom, so that I don't make too big of an ass of myself?"

Before Mary answers, she looks over at Mario. When he gives Mary an approving nod. Evan rolls his eyes. Still, he puts his arm around Mary's waist as they walk out.

I turn to Mario. "Let me guess," I say. "Mary is to be your eyes and ears on us."

Mario's mouth drops open. "You must be psychic."

"And you must be psycho," I retort. "This is a very

dangerous mission! You saw the carnage in Granny Doo's diner! Eagle and Snake doesn't mess around."

"She'll be perfectly safe," Mario insists.

"She'll be in the field! That wasn't our deal. She's still too much of a civilian to recognize when she's in over her head."

He sighs. "If it makes you feel more comfortable, I'll be there too. I promise to keep an eye on her."

Despite knowing how that will upset Evan, I mumble, "Good. Because if anything happens to her, at least I'll know where to find you."

Mario sighs. "I've been duly warned."

My cell pings. There's a message from Lee:

**They won! Ice cream and then sleepover at my place.
We'll drop them off in the morning.**

I text back:

**Let them know that Jack, Mary, Evan, and I will be out of
town from tomorrow morning through the weekend.
We'll call tomorrow evening to check in.**

Lee answers with:

**Will do. I suppose that means Evan and Mary have
worked out their differences?**

I respond:

It's a livable truce.

Lee answers with:

I can relate. Great luck to you, sweet Donna.

Curious, Jack looks down at my phone. "Fan mail?"

I shift it away. "Just… Lee. The girls won their game. He's hosting the team to a sleepover."

He smirks. "Like I said, fan mail."

Mario shakes his head. "You Craigs! You'll always be my favorite soap opera!"

Our glares chase him out the door.

7

Selfies

A SELFIE IS A PHOTO YOU TAKE OF YOURSELF, USUALLY WITH *your cell phone.*

Of course, you can take it with another device—say, a Tablet of some form, like an iPad or Surface.

You can even do a selfie with others in the picture with you. (Of course, then it's not strictly a selfie, but a "group-sie," right?)

If you take a selfie with someone you don't like, consider downloading one of the many apps that will erase items in photos, as if they were never there. It's the best sort of cosmetic surgery: with one quick swipe, the pain in your ass is gone.

"Ow-Ow-AH-WHOOOOOOOO! TIME TO GET DOWN! To Par-TAY!" Lyle Greenwich's coyote howl proves he's living up to his party-hardy frat boy persona, which includes an uncanny resemblance, both in face and physique, to John Belushi. Like him, his posse—generously breasted gals hanging on guys trying too hard to outdo each other with head-butts and forehead can crushes—are decked out in togas and dancing to their resident DJ's thundering mix of good-time oldies.

Thank God the plane chartered for the ten Facey contestants coming from the Los Angeles metro area—an Airbus 350-900XLR— is large enough that those of us who don't share Lyle's zest for life can find some quieter corners for the five-hour flight to Baltimore-Washington International Airport. The plane's myriad break-out spaces have different seating configurations. One area has numerous pods sporting a single captain's chair with a console and monitor worthy of a Federation starship. In another area, ergonomic chairs surround several tables laden with healthy snacks and bottles of sparkling water. Lyle's hoe-down takes place in a sunken plexiglass room lined by a humongous U-shaped couch.

As per our covers, my Acme mission team arrived separately in the FaceStaTweet-hired limos that picked us up from Acme safehouses that were used as our fake addresses. Evan and I arrived as a pair, as did Arnie and Mary. Dominic, Jody, and Abu came together since she's formally listed as the consulting producer to both.

All Acme undercover operatives have altered their appearances. There are wigs for everyone, as well as facial hair for the men. Besides a short platinum wig with spiked neon green tips, Mary opted for a fake tattoo on her neck, and a nose ring: two items that I've vetoed in real life.

That's okay. Spies live for their cosplay.

Mary and Evan wear non-prescription eyeglasses.

They've also been fitted with Acme's ear buds and special see-all contact lenses, in colors that change their eyes' natural hue. It took a few lessons, but they seem to have gotten the hang of seeing something other than what their eyes tell them is real.

Jack arrived alone. He sits in another section of the cabin with two other potential FaceStaTweet investors: a banker named Claudia Whitlock and the renowned venture capitalist, Jonathan Morrow. The Facey Award's event director, Hansley Bardot, is also onboard. For some reason, she thinks nothing of playing with my husband's jacket lapel. I assume she appreciates the cut of his brand-new suit, a bespoke Alexander Amosu. Can't say I blame her. It's blended from three wools, took eighty hours and over fifty-thousand stitches to create, and costs ninety-five thousand dollars, according to the receipt that was enclosed in its hanging bag.

I wonder how she'd feel if she knew it was confiscated from the wardrobe of a Dutch financier who had the temerity to siphon off the investments he made on his government's behalf? When his indiscretions were discovered, it was determined that the best way to keep the scandal at bay was to bury the loss—and the financier.

Acme was hired to ensure his fatal heart attack while he attended an international investment conference here in Los Angeles. The exterminator was Jack. After the hit, he couldn't just walk out of the hotel in his waiter duds, now could he? The fact that he and the target are both suit size 40 Slim was serendipitous.

Jack calls it the best piece in his "Dead Man Walking" wardrobe. Ah, the spoils of war.

For the Facey plane, we arrived late to the tarmac on purpose. Emma's team hacked the passenger manifest and texted it to us, along with the suspects' newly-created dossiers. That way, we can put names to faces as we make friends and weed out enemies. Before I sit down, I look around to see who I now recognize.

Besides the loutish Lyle, another contestant in Dominic's category is onboard: a home stylist named Mina Concha. This caftan-wearing earth mother's stock in trade is cozy abodes showcasing soft-focus photos of fuzzy rugs in front of well-lit fireplaces, or comfortable nooks lit by sparkly lights or flickering candles. Invariably, her photos include a shot of her hands sheathed in fingerless gloves and wrapped around some mug of steaming goodness: say, bone broth dotted with bits of basil, or thick Spanish hot cocoa. In Mina's videos, Indian guitar music accompanies her husky voice as she spouts New Age platitudes. For the most part, she stays off-camera. Until now I'd assumed it was part of her mystique. But then I realize that her actions—hanging back, blushing when spoken to, profusely thanking the flight attendants for even the smallest kindness—are that of an innately shy person.

So, why has she chosen a profession where you must be continually in the public eye?

Also on the plane is Jessica Patchett, a lifestyle contestant who bills herself as "the feminist folklorist." Her videos are short stories that, as she puts it, "honors extraordinary women leading everyday lives." She practically bristles when Arnie plops down on the table beside her and greets her with, "How's tricks?"

Mary, who has retrieved two glasses of sparkling water

from a flight attendant, offers one to Jessica. It's the perfect ice breaker. As my daughter gushes over Jessica's videos, Arnie goes to work, hacking Jessica's computer via the plane's WiFi signal, then scanning it for clues that she is a viable suspect. In fact, every Acme team member's cell phone is equipped with an app that runs hacks on all WiFi-receiving mobile devices within a ten-foot radius. It then relays the devices' contacts, texts, and files to Arnie's computer, allowing him to do a deep dive through this intel, flagging anything of interest for ComInt's closer scrutiny.

The trick is that we've got to spend a minimum of five minutes beside the hacked device. A five-hour flight will give us plenty of time for this.

In the meantime, Abu, Jack, Dominic, Mary, Evan, and I will figure out reasons to converse with each of the other suspects, or at least sit beside them for five minutes. What someone doesn't say is just as important as what they unwittingly divulge via their devices.

Abu is already chatting up the only other dance contestants on the plane: Eric and Erica Grisham, who film their perfectly choreographed sensually charged dance routines to various pop tunes on the Hollywood Walk of Fame. Eric is bristling because Erica is flirting with Abu, who is enjoying every minute of it.

Dominic and Jody have squeezed themselves onto the U-shaped sofa in Lyle's sunken play pit. I'd like to think that my British teammate is trying to hack Lyle's phone, but since he's not close enough to Lyle to use his cell as a transmitter, my guess is that it's to appear in enough posts uploaded by Lyle's guests' posts that it will introduce him to their followers and that they'll follow him too.

What an egomaniac.

Obviously miffed by this too, Lyle shakes an unopened Champagne bottle and takes aim at Dominic. When he uncorks it, Dominic is bathed in its fizzy spray. His sputtering epitaphs, loud enough to drown out the music, are caught by every mobile aimed in his direction.

Yep, he got his wish. He's an internet sensation.

Make that a laughingstock.

When he stalks off, Jody follows him, shooting a finger at Lyle.

The only other passenger on the plane who shares my category is the world-renowned restaurant chef, Grady McDougall. He's quite a busy guy, what with three restaurants in Los Angeles, one in San Francisco, another in Napa, and yet another in New York. Grady sits with his entourage of stylists and producers around a large table filled with picnic baskets from which they sample a feast of delicacies he's brought onboard. I'm sure the food—and Grady—will take center stage in the various posts and videos that will be posted on Grady's FaceStaTweet account throughout the day. When he sees me enter the cabin, he smirks, then pokes one of his many sycophants, who has been tapping away furiously on an iPad.

The dude looks up, spots me, then laughs uproariously.

When I pass the creep, I spill my complimentary Champagne on his shoulder.

When he yelps, I coo, "Oops, my bad."

As I walk by Grady, he declares, "Touché, Miss Delish."

I ignore him—for now. This kind of guy likes women who play hard to get.

The overhead speaker crackles with the voice of our pilot. After welcoming us aboard, he then apologizes for being late on take-off. "We're still waiting for one other contestant," he explains. "Ah! Here he is now!"

As the latecomer comes aboard, I almost drop my Champagne glass:

It's Cheever.

Well, well, well. Penelope wasn't shoving malarky after all!

Yikes, and speaking of the devil—

She follows him into the cabin.

Just then, Mary looks up and sees her too. My daughter's face loses all its color. She turns, angling herself in such a way that they can't see her. When Mary glances over at me, I nod toward the back of the plane.

She skedaddles in that direction.

She ducks into one of the smaller conference rooms. Evan and I follow her in.

After shutting the door, I tap my ear bud. "Emma, it would have been great to have gotten a heads-up about the Bings!"

"Sorry, Don. It took us by surprise too," Emma admits. "According to FaceStaTweet's latest press release on the event, Cheever was a last-minute addition. One of the other gaming streamer contestants dropped out."

"Well, at least we can eliminate him as a target," I mutter. "At worst, he's just a nuisance."

Mary groans. "It'll be awful if he discovers I'm

onboard! What if he tries to interview me? Besides ruining any chance to clear my name, I'll blow Acme's cover."

"Before you panic, you've got to remember that you don't look like Mary Craig anymore," I remind her. To prove this contention, I point to the mirror on the wall.

Mary stares back at herself. Finally, she nods, though she's still shaking. "But…what if one of the Bings recognizes my voice?"

"If you happen to be around them, keep mum. Remember: you're just a lowly assistant. Cheever and Mrs. Bing are here for the glory of hanging with other influencers," Evan replies.

"Ten to one she'll gravitate to Grady McDougall. And since Cheever is a man-whore in the making, Lyle's party will be hard for him to resist," I add.

The tension goes out of Mary's shoulders. "Yes, yes… you're right."

When Evan takes her hand, she holds tight to him.

I don't blame her. Missions build trust.

In time, Mary says, "We shouldn't be seen with each other. Why don't I duck out first? After a while, you can follow."

"Go for it," I reply.

In a flash, she's gone.

I turn to Evan. "I don't think Cheever knows what you normally look like. Even if he does, he wouldn't recognize you now. Since Dominic went off to sulk after Lyle's little trick on him, why don't you infiltrate that jerk's party?"

"Will do."

"Try chatting up one of the girls. That way, you're in

the thick of things. The closer she is to Lyle, the better. That way, you can hack and transmit his intel to Arnie."

He frowns. "But… what if Mary sees me flirting? I wouldn't want her to get the wrong idea."

"If she does, then she's not cut out for this business, so it's a win-win for you. Trust me, Jack and I have to flirt with others all the time."

Evan guffaws. "And you call that a win-win?"

"No. I call it trust." What I don't mention is that, as a couple in a loving relationship, it's the hardest part of our job.

Evan must see this in my eyes because he pats me on the shoulder before heading out the door.

I'm just about to follow him when someone enters: Grady. The dome on the silver tray he holds in one hand is raised, revealing various savory appetizers. "A peace offering, from your greatest admirer."

I stiffen. "You have an interesting way of showing it. When I walk into a room, I rarely elicit sniggers."

"Believe me, Miss Delish, I didn't mean to put you down. It was a groan of love from a smitten fan. My producer, Justin Teasdale, knows of my little crush. He was just as taken aback at your entrance as me."

I don't lose my pout until after I flip on the hack app. Then I'm all smiles. "What say I get your apology on video so that my fans can see that you're not such a meanie after all?"

He angles his head so that the pose is ideal, then he smiles for the camera. I walk over, arm extended, so that we're both in the shot. "Yum! Which would you suggest I try first?"

"I know the perfect appetizer," Grady murmurs.

The next thing I know he's got me in a lip lock—

Make that a tongue tussle—

Okay, I'll bite—

And hard.

His yelp is stifled until I let go of his tongue, at which point I take a stuffed mushroom cap and pop it into his mouth.

Grady isn't prepared for it, let alone for the rapid speed in which our plane taxis down the runway. Just as we have lift-off, the amuse bouche gets stuck in Grady's throat. He staggers back, dropping the tray.

This isn't a sanctioned hit, and heaven knows I don't want it to look like I had it out for my competition, so I'm left with the only alternative: giving him the Heimlich maneuver.

I put down my cellphone, but not so far away that it can't keep scanning and transmitting from Grady's cell to Arnie's computer.

The third Heimlich's the charm. As the mushroom goes flying, I notice that my FaceStaTweet likes are popping like crazy.

It's just at that moment that Grady's producer, Justin, chooses to stick his head through the door. He frowns, obviously annoyed to see his boss with me. "Oh, there you are, big guy! We've been looking all over for you."

Grady waves him away. He's still staring at me, awed. "Miss Delish just saved my life!"

"Really?" Justin scrutinizes me. "How about when we land, we'll thank her with a gift basket of Grady's Goodies? Considering the swill she dishes out, I'm sure she'll appreciate it."

"Don't bother," I mutter.

"But…I insist!" Grady stammers.

"You heard the man. And since his wish is my command…" Justin shrugs. "You'll be tempted to eat it all in one night, but I wouldn't suggest it. I know how you ladies like to look svelte and gorgeous, and the camera already adds five or six pounds." He twists his head to stare at my ass.

I squelch the urge to lop off the easiest five or six pounds on his carcass: his swelled head.

Despite Justin's bum's rush, Grady stares back at me with goo-goo eyes.

If those two are any indication, I sure know how to win friends and instigate frenemies.

I wonder how many likes I'd have gotten if Grady had choked to death? I guess we'll never know.

Although, I'd be willing to bet it would have won me the Facey.

I ROAM THROUGH THE CABIN IN THE HOPE OF AVOIDING ANY of the Family Bing—

Only to discover Arnie chitchatting with Cheever. They're trading notes on their favorite *Tower of Power* shortcuts in a whole different language than any I've heard.

Good to her word, Mary is nowhere near them.

When I catch Arnie's eye, he winks, then gives a slight

shake of his head. I guess it's his way of saying he's hacked Cheever's computer and found nothing of consequence.

Heck, I could have told him that.

So, where is Mary?

Certainly not where I finally find her:

She and Lyle are making out between gulps of Champagne.

How?…

Why?…

Evan may have a girl on each arm, but both eyes are on Lyle's hand, which is inching up beneath Mary's midriff top.

In a second, Evan has shrugged off the toga'ed tootsies. Both fists clenched, Evan starts over to Lyle—

But I grab him and pull him away and into an empty conference room. "What the hell do you think you're doing?" I hiss.

"You're her mother! Don't you care that she's being mauled by that douchebag?"

"When have you known Mary not to be able to take care of herself?" Even as I say this, I'm fighting the impulse to pull that creep off my daughter and neuter him to boot.

"Like, maybe now? He's handing out roofies to his buddies as party favors! They've been pairing off all night in the smaller compartments." He glances up, then around frantically.

"They're gone—Mary and Lyle!"

Shite.

"I'll go left, you go right. Call if you find her, and I'll do the same." I grab his arm. "Evan, if you run across anyone being assaulted, stop it!"

"You better believe I will." He's off in a flash.

And so am I.

I'VE PICKED THE LOCKS ON SEVEN CUBICLES: NO MARY.

But when I come across women who are too drugged up to know who's mauling them, the stun gun tucked in my pocket gives a stunning message to their perpetrators. After I drag the victims out of the room and into one of the individual pods so that they can sleep safely, I lock the door so that the perpetrator can't escape the rape room.

I've just completed my search-and-save mission on all the cubicles on my side when Emma whispers: "I've tapped into the plane's security feed and downloaded video on the roofie distribution. Since interstate transport was involved, I forwarded the video along with a list of the perpetrators and their victims to the Baltimore FBI office, which will meet the flight. Then, from Jack's cell, I've texted the lead flight attendant and the pilot the details of the assaults, and what private rooms to lock down for the investigators. The flight staff is already zip-tying the perpetrators in one of the larger bays, which will be used as a holding pen. I don't think FaceStaTweet will protect the rapists. The company will cooperate if only to hush up what happened on its watch, especially since there are investors onboard, and one—Jack Craig, of Acme —has already notified the authorities."

"Thanks for taking care of this, Emma." Even if Lyle isn't Eagle and Snake, he's a creep who should be in jail.

I see Mary and Evan headed my way. The last thing my daughter looks like is a damsel in distress. Instead, she's smiling triumphantly.

I search her face, then Evan's. "Did Lyle try to…you know…"

Mary shrugs. "He couldn't get it up if he tried—not after I exchanged Champagne flutes with him. He went out like a light."

Ah, that old trick! I've used it myself.

Turning to Evan, Mary adds, "Next time, don't barge in, okay? It's not that I don't appreciate your old-fashioned attempt at valor but it's time you realize that I'm not totally helpless."

Evan frowns. "If you're saying I should let you traipse off with a rapist without a second thought, you've got another think coming!"

"Like you, I saw what was happening. You did the right thing, Evan—helping those women. But I did the right thing too, by completing my mission and transmitting Lyle's intel to Arnie, then getting out of there as fast as I could." Mary flails her hands. "You must give me the space to prove I can take care of myself. Is that too much to ask?"

Evan smolders in silence. Finally: "Yeah, okay. If you want to get killed, I don't need to blame myself for caring."

He stalks off.

Frustrated, Mary shakes her head. "He just doesn't get it."

"He's worried about losing you."

"If he keeps it up, he will." She heads off in the other direction.

Ah, young love.

I look at my watch. By now we should be flying over Colorado.

As if reading my mind, Emma whispers in my ear: "We've only hacked a quarter of the mobile devices on the plane. At that rate, I don't know if we'll get to all of them before we land. You know, one of the stunned creeps could be Eagle and Snake. No better time to scan their cells than when they're hogtied."

In other words, I'd better get moving.

A long flight just got longer.

I head down the corridor toward the assaulters' holding pen—

Only to come within a few feet away of Penelope—

And Jack—

Who waves me over. "Oh, look… there she is now," he exclaims.

What the hell?

Still, I turn my frown upside down and saunter over as if I don't have a care in the world. I hold out my hand to Jack—

Who takes it and clasps it to Penelope's.

"Miss Delish, I'm Jack Craig and I'm a big fan," Jack

says. "But my friend here, Penelope Bing, is an even bigger one."

Ack! Proof positive that celebrity is both a blessing and a curse…

"Is that so?" My purr drips with Southern-fried charm.

"I'm… beside myself!" Penelope gushes. "Would you mind if we took a selfie together?"

The next thing I know, she's cradled her head on my neck.

Yuck…

Pee-hew! What the hell kind of perfume is she wearing? "My, my. Your perfume is…"

"Divine, isn't it? My son's new sponsor created it—and named it after him. It'll premiere at the tournament. It's called '*Odeur Puante.*' Cheever—my son—came up with the name. Well, the English version. The sponsor suggested putting a French twist on it." She shrugs. "Classy, isn't it? And all Cheever must do is mention it during the tournament with the sales link, and it will sell a million bottles! And the best part of all? We get twenty percent of *every tiny bottle sold.*"

"Lucky you," I mutter.

"You betcha!" Joyously, she yanks my neck closer.

Even as I smile, I hold my breath.

"Say cheese puff!" After snapping the shot, Penelope adds, "I was just telling Jack that I know his wife would be so *jealous* to see us together."

"Who… *You*? And…um, Mr. Craig?" *Now I've heard everything!*

"I didn't mean me. I meant you!" Playfully, she punches my arm.

I force myself not to punch her back—not so playfully, like say, in the face. Instead I mutter, "Why, pray tell?"

"But of course he can't help but admire you. To a starving man, a great chef is better than a great lay." Her lousy joke comes with an elbow poke to my side.

I return the elbow poke—*only harder*—when Jack inserts himself between us.

Yikes! Bad timing.

Despite doubling over in pain, he gasps, "Ah, ladies, you sure know how to make a man feel appreciated."

"Mr. Craig doesn't look like he's starving, so Mrs. Craig must be doing something right," I retort.

Penelope looks heavenward. "Are you kidding? I guess the only good thing to come out of having a wife who burns everything whenever she's near an oven is that Jack loses his appetite. Just look at this slim, sexy, well-cut piece of prime beefcake." She pats Jack's chest.

More to the point, she rubs it seductively.

Grrrr….

Jack must know what I'm thinking because he's chortling through his pain.

We'll see who laughs last.

Key Performance Indicator

THE METRIC USED TO MEASURE THE PROGRESS OF YOUR SOCIAL media goals is called a Key Performance Indicator, or KPI.

For example, if your social media goal is to increase your viewer reach, the solution is simple: more intriguing posts that inspire others to repost them, or link back to your post.

Or it may be used to increase awareness to your brand. Solution: more advertising on the platforms specifically honed to your target audiences.

A Key Performance Indicator that you are a great spouse and parent: the number of kisses, hugs, and "I love you" declarations received on any given day.

There is truly no need to post such accolades on social media.

"WOW! TALK ABOUT SCORING A REALLY SWEET SUITE!" Arnie's jaw is gaping open after his tour of Jack's digs on the Prince Charles, which, thanks to Emma's reservation hacking, shares an adjoining door with my more modest room. "Sunken living room, deluxe kitchen, formal dining room, terrace with water view, a hot tub that fits six—and an Eastern King bed?" Arnie shakes his head in disbelief. "Why isn't the number one gaming streamer in digs like this?"

Abu snorts. "Who, Cheever? My guess is that he's got this joint's twin on the floor below."

"Arnie is right. The difference between the rest of our rooms and Jack's is egregious," Dominic sniffs. "Why is everything nowadays about showing one the money?"

"The saying is 'show *me* the money,'" I counter.

Only, in this case, it's Hansley Bardot who wants something—and she wants it from Jack. By the way she was salivating over him on the plane, it's obvious that cash isn't the only kind of infusion she wants from him.

Mary chuckles. "Either way, the phrase is totally old school."

Jack grins. "Nothing wrong with old school if it looks like this."

"Quit pouting, people." From Jack's cell, Ryan's voice booms through the room, like a deity scorned. "Emma, fill them in on ComInt's analysis of the data collected on the plane."

Emma begins: "The influencers on the plane who were cleared were Cheever Bing, Mina Concha, and Tremor. The financial VIPS, Jonathan Morrow and Carson Whitlock, came out clean too. However, we found four cells with FaceStaTweet accounts that include public messages with the exact same wording sent from another account that was also used to communicate with Randy and Candy

Murphy. At the time the message was sent by the mystery account, it was then answered by the accounts in receipt. Additionally, the accounts were within proximity of a national security breach. Since the messages were obviously in code, ComInt is deciphering now."

"Well, that's a start," Dominic declares. "Who did we snare in our trap?"

"You, specifically, snared no one," Ryan retorts. "You were too busy pouting over Lyle's little joke. One suspect came from Donna's intel, two from Jack's, and the fourth from Mary."

Mary squeaks with delight. "Way to go, Team Craig!"

"This isn't a pep rally, young lady," Ryan barks.

No one says a word. Mary stares down at her feet—

Until Evan's snort earns him a death stare from her. To his credit, he doesn't turn away from it.

She peeks out when Ryan adds: "Donna's intel came from Grady McDougall's cell, and Mary's intel proved that Lyle is involved. However, the two transmissions from Jack came from unidentified accounts."

Jack shakes his head, stymied. "It can't be too hard to figure out. All of that time I was conversing with the investors and the event's director, Hansley."

"And don't forget Penelope Bing," I tease.

"Penelope's cell was clean, as was Hansley's," Emma replies. "Jack, at some point during that long flight you must have stepped away from them."

Jack shrugs. "I'll do my best to remember who I stood beside for at least a good five minutes."

"In the meantime, Arnie will be reviewing the transmissions' timetables to help you pinpoint it. As for Lyle, he'll be out of commission for the duration of the event. His orgy already has him in trouble with the Feds, which allows Mario to put the squeeze on him. As for you, Donna: McDougall was working hard to get friendly with you. I'd suggest you let him."

I don't react. I can't. *Not in front of Mary.*

Is she smart enough to put two and two together?

"Hansley Bardot gave each of you the event's itinerary," Ryan reminds us. "Tonight you'll be meeting with the press and fans while squeezing in live video reels. The moment the event goes live, likes and comments for your stills and reels will be tallied. This will be going on throughout the weekend. Whereas this activity is the icing, the cake is the event's ninety-minute live-stream finale, which takes place on Saturday evening. Each contestant will be allowed one last post, based on a specific topic that you'll select at random. The highest scorer in each category wins a prize of fifty thousand dollars. But the top Facey prize—two hundred and fifty thousand dollars—goes to the overall winner. Of course, sponsors will be wooing the influencers too, even the runners-up."

"But there is also a lot of social time built into the schedule with those competitors who have yet to be vetted. You'll find their dossiers in Acme's secure cloud," Emma interjects. "Abu, besides Eric and Erica, the other dance acts are Joe the Poser, who mimics other dancers and their routines to a tee, even down to their costumes. The Lóng Twins, who dance all sorts of styles, from ballroom to hip-hop to tap to swing; and the influencer known as LOL Pasadena. Her specialty is nineteen-fifties and sixties pop and rock-and-roll dance steps, interspersed with current club moves."

"On it," Abu says.

"Arnie, though Cheever and Tremor were cleared, there are two other gamers to vet. Their names are Fantasy Fling and The Detonator."

"I've been tracking all of them," he assures her. "And I'm happy to report, I'm leading all the others in points—except for that pompous little jerk, Cheever."

"We're not here to win, remember? We're here to take down Eagle and Snake," Ryan reminds him.

"Which brings up another question." Arnie hesitates, then: "What if one of us wins? By that I mean, do we get to keep the prize money?"

"Isn't saving your country from a terrorist attack enough of a win for you?" Ryan retorts.

No one answers.

Ryan sighs. "I'd prefer to give bonuses for each terrorist we apprehend."

Abu breaks out in a happy dance.

"Shall we continue?" Emma says. "Donna, be on the lookout for Sweet Meat. He's from Memphis."

"Let me guess: he's all about the barbecue."

She chuckles. "You've got that right. And there's also Stewie—"

"Don't tell me," I mutter, "Insta-Pot meals?"

"Yep—not only easy-peasy, but divine!" Emma exclaims. "And, finally, there's Bake It or Fake it. Like you, she focuses on short cuts on quick meals."

"Gotcha."

"Dominic, the lifestyle competitors yet to be vetted are

Sammy French, a realtor who sells mega-Mansions, and the super-model, Alana Partain."

"Ah!... Well, the latter may be somewhat awkward. We were once an item—for all of an evening."

"Use it to your advantage," Ryan insists. "Tell her she's the one who got away, yadda yadda, yadda—"

Dominic frowns. "Yes, well, it is the 'yadda yadda yadda' part that may be disconcerting."

Ryan sighs. "In what way?"

"Alana doesn't just stop at three yaddas. She is more inclined to yadda all night..." Dominic's voice trails off. "And...at this point...I am indisposed to extracurricular activity."

All side chatter stops.

Finally Ryan declares, "Clear the room folks—*except for Dominic.*"

Jack hands Dominic his cell and points to the bedroom.

Dominic takes it—and the hint, shutting the door behind him.

While everyone else files out of the room, Mary and I stay behind. Evan hangs back too, but he never glances Mary's way. From what I can tell, he's been ignoring Mary since the incident with Lyle.

Mary turns to Jack and me. "A quick question. Was Dominic talking about...well, what I *think* he was talking about?"

"If you're asking whether Dominic is informing Ryan that he'd like to forgo any honeytrap activities, the answer is yes," Evan informs her. He turns to me. "Isn't that what you call it?"

Before I can answer, Mary retorts, "I wasn't asking you. The question was for my parents." Her face is bright red.

Jack and I exchange glances. Guessing rightly that I can't find the right words to explain this part of my job to my daughter, Jack finally says: "He's right."

"But… You see…" I stumble to find the right words. The only thing I can think of says nothing while saying everything: "It's all in a day's work."

Mary nods stiffly. "Ah. I see. Well, I'd better get ready for the influencer reception." Her pace is casual, but I know my daughter well enough to gauge the concern in her voice.

But whatever it is, she doesn't want to discuss it in front of Evan.

"Is there something we can do for you, Evan?" Jack asks.

"Yes. It's about…." He glances in my direction. "I got a request from Mario, but it… it will affect my role in the mission going forward."

"Donna, maybe you should get ready for the reception as well," Jack suggests.

"I can take a hint." I salute him as I go into my adjoining room.

But after shutting the door, I fight the urge to put a cup to the wall and listen in.

Need to know basis, my ass…

The Prince Charles's ballroom is a cacophony of laughter and ecstatic conversation. For influencers, the event is akin to the movie industry's Oscars, and they've dressed accordingly. Flamboyant flair is what their followers have come to expect of them, and they won't be disappointed.

The Faceys has provided what their followers consider the ultimate photo op: group hugs with their honored peers, which are immediately uploaded to their individual FaceStaTweet accounts.

In other words, it's the ultimate circle jerk.

Jody has the duty of capturing the images of all of Acme team's undercover influencers. She moves fast, thanks to the side slit in her stunningly beautiful electric-blue gown, which keeps her legs free enough to stay on the move.

Dominic for one is mesmerized by it. But he heard Ryan loud and clear and is cozying up to Alana. What makes it all too obvious that she's reveling in having their relationship renewed? Easy answer: She's loosened the bowtie on Dominic's tux so that she can lead him around by it. If he even glances at another woman, she puts him in a choke hold.

He longs to gaze at Jody but he's afraid he'll pass out.

Jack and I stand on opposite sides of the ballroom. We're talking to each other on a private channel via our ear buds.

"Where's your new bestie, Penelope?" I tease.

Jack shrugs. "This place is hook-up central. With Cheever being such a celeb, even saying you've made it with his mom will afford some desperate fan some caché."

I scan the room. "Nope, you're wrong. She's standing in the far corner with Grady's producer, Justin."

Jack's lips barely move as his eyes go to the couple in question. "Ha! Funny. That dude didn't strike me as desperate. Then again, as hard as these influencers work, their producers seem to have no lives whatsoever. I guess that makes him easy pickings for Mrs. Bing."

"It must be the other way around. Look, he's got his hand on her ass."

"Ah! You're right!" He takes a closer look. "Interesting. She doesn't seem to be enjoying herself."

"I'm sure she feels her Cheever card earns her a celebrity boink. It must be disappointing to discover she's just another face in the crowd—or, in social media parlance, another 'like' in the followsphere."

"Too bad Miss Delish has Justin's boss wrapped around her little finger." Jack's brow rises up as if daring me to deny it.

I can't. Even now, Grady is lurking just within my peripheral vision, hoping I'll see him and save him from Bake It and Fake It, who's trying very hard to show him her tramp stamp, which looks like a baguette standing up straight between two wheels of brie.

Could she be any more obvious?

"The longer I play hard to get, the more I'll get from Grady," I insist. "At least, that's what I'm telling Ryan—for as long as I can, what with Mary now in the mix."

"No matter how badly it bugs us personally, you and I both know we can't dodge our roles in this mission forever." Jack's voice is heavy with weariness. "On a more pleasant topic, how many transmissions have you sent? Enough to call it a night?"

"I think so. I've sent one from everyone in my category:

I cornered Sweet Meat first. What a doll! He gave me some super meat-tenderizing tips! And, man, he even smells like hickory. In fact, I've been invited to his hotel room tomorrow afternoon. He's going to be barbecuing ribs on his terrace and all the influencers in our category are invited to taste them."

Jack chuckles. "If ComInt reports he's clean, consider skipping his little hoedown. That dress is practically sewn on. You wouldn't want to bust a seam."

I stick out my tongue at him. "Hardee-har-har! You're right about me not going in this get-up, but for the wrong reasons. First off, the dress is white, so I wouldn't dare get it near barbecue. Secondly, he wants me to bet the dress on who'll end up with the most points."

"What's he offering in return?" Jack asks.

"A year of meals showcasing his special barbecue sauces, delivered weekly."

Jack nods grudgingly. "He's slim enough for that gown. But the cut is all wrong. He's got shoulders like a linebacker! Still, the offer to feed our ravenous family isn't to be taken lightly. Did you agree to the bet?"

"Heck, no! The final and best reason to pass is that that this dress is classic nineteen-thirties couture—in other words, very expensive!"

My gown is an ivory white lace slip dress, cut on the bias, with a matching fitted bolero jacket that ties at the neck with a bow, creating a keyhole neckline. The sleeves puff slightly and end just below the elbow. Petals of lace flow down its see-through skirt and edge its backless bodice, all the way to the shoulders. I'm wearing a platinum blond wig cut in a wavy pixie of spit curls.

"You do look great, doll." Jack sighs. "Wish I could hold you in my arms now."

"So do I."

My voice is so soft that Jack is compelled to look over. He touches his heart with his right hand: his secret signal that he loves me.

He got it from Mary. He noticed that she does this whenever she gets off the phone with Evan when he's away at college.

I wonder if, like me, he's thinking of them right now.

Since I'm done with my homework, I nod toward the elevator banks. Jack winks his approval: his promise is to help me strip out of this frilly retro concoction as soon as we get up to our rooms.

But just as I take my leave, I notice Hansley sidling over to Jack. Her role as the event's director is to work the room all night. I guess it's quitting time for her too because she's got her head on his shoulder. He nods and smiles at what she's saying, then allows her to take his hand and pull him out of the ballroom.

What the heck? She was cleared as a suspect, so he no longer has to kowtow to her!

Hmmm…

"Are you going to ignore me all night?" Grady murmurs in my ear.

He's right. While I traded recipes with Stewie and grilling tips with Sweet Meat, I pretended not to see him. I smile up at him now. "Not at all. In fact, I wanted to ask you if you've fully recovered from the bruising I gave you when I saved your life." Gently, I lay my hand on his abdomen, never taking my eyes off his.

At that moment I notice Mary staring at me.

Oh, heck…

When I turn away, Grady grabs my hand. "Hey, don't stop now. Things were just getting interesting. Besides, I never got the chance to thank you—personally." He looks around. "This shindig is thinning out. What say you and I find a nice quiet balcony and watch the sun set over the bay?"

"You've got a lousy sense of direction. The bay faces east."

"Oh… did I say set?" He grins wickedly. "I meant watch it *rise*. The night is young, right?" He pulls me in close, for a kiss.

Instinctively I look over at Mary.

I'll never forget the look of shock on her face.

All in a day's work…

Who do I think I'm kidding? My daughter just saw me kiss a perfect stranger.

And she knows why.

If she put two and two together as to what Dominic must do for his country, seeing my pick-up must make me a complete zero in her eyes.

She'll never see me the same way again: as a loving wife of the father she adores.

I'M TOO NUMB FROM MY SHAME TO STOP GRADY FROM PAWING me in the elevator.

When the door chimes open to his floor, the kissing

continues, even as he pulls my almost comatose body down the hall toward his suite.

Somehow, I've got to get out of this predicament—and this damn mission…

With my daughter's respect intact.

I stop short. Shoving him away, I exclaim: "Grady, I—"

A door flings open and six giggling girls come running out. They are accompanied by four men, a teen boy, and two women:

Janie, Trisha, four other friends from their soccer team—

And Jeff!

As well as Lee, his assistant, Eve Green, the girls's coach, Kendra Middleton, and his Secret Service detail, including Porter—

And Aunt Phyllis.

What the heck are they doing here? ….

I grab Grady by the collar and smack his lips back onto mine.

Seeing us, the girls gasp, and then giggle all the harder.

"Girls, it's not polite to stare. Keep moving," Kendra's command only makes them snicker louder.

Suddenly, Janie squeals, "Oh, my God! That's *Grady McDougall!*"

"And…*Miss Delish!*" Trisha adds. "I love it when one of her recipes goes all cray-cray! I'm going to get an autograph!"

Oh my God is right! My own daughter recognizes me!…

Wait! Not me, but my alias…

But…if she—and Jeff—get close enough…

They are close now. *Much too close.*

Close enough to see that it's me in a lip lock with a man who isn't her father…

"Everyone in the elevator—now!" Porter commands. "There will be plenty of other influencers to ogle downstairs."

The kids grumble, but they do as he demands.

As they walk off, I hear Aunt Phyllis say, "You don't have to be so snippy, Porter. Now that I'm an influential, my posse has the right to get up close and personal with those folks."

Jeff sighs, "Aunt Phyllis, for the fifth time, it's 'influencer,' not influen-*tial!*"

Aunt Phyllis giggles. "L-O-L, Jeff! Remember? I'm L-O-L'ing right now, so what I say goes—" The door closes.

Dammit, I've had enough of this.

I pull a tiny perfume spritzer from my clutch. This time when I pull away from Grady, I hold my breath. His eyes are still closed but his nostrils are wide open for the sleeping gas sprayed his way.

He slumps to the floor, snoring.

I search for his room card: Not in his jacket…

Ah, in his pants pocket. But I recoil when I realize it's up against something hard: his stiffened fifth appendage.

Gah!

I can't leave him out in the hall while I search his room. What if the girls come back this way?

So instead, I drag him in, then on through the living room, and into the bedroom. With a grunt, I lift him once more, onto the bed.

He groans as he lands on his back.

While he cuts z's like a buzzsaw, I search the room. The computer is in the room's safe. An Acme app reads its pass code with no problem. While the data is being transmitted to ComInt, I check his suitcases for anything that might detonate, blow-up, or shoot to kill.

Nothing like that.

What I do find doesn't surprise me: an interesting cache of sex toys: a silicone ball gag. A couple of floggers. Nipple clamps. Wrist and ankle restraints. A leather hog tie. A studded collar on a leash—

Ah, and here's something interesting: an "electro-play wand." It doesn't pack the wallop of my stun gun, but it is cuter.

Nay, I don't want him to think I'm cute. I want him to know I mean business.

He's also got a Classic Wüsthof Classic 6-inch cleaver and an eight-inch Shun Dual Core Kiritsuke chef knife, but that's to be expected. Is there anything sexier than a man who knows his way around tools? If they're kitchen tools, then I say no. One day he'll make some little lady very happy—

During conjugal visits at some Federal penitentiary.

I hate to disappoint him, but she won't be me.

I guess he'll never forgive me for being the person who puts him there.

When everything is back where it belongs, I strip him down and tether him to the bed with the restraints and the leash. After putting the ball gag in his mouth, with my lipstick I draw a kiss on his cheek.

Then I sneak out.

I decide to take the fire stairs as opposed to the elevator. Now that the fans are arriving, the last thing I need is to run into some.

And then it hits me—

Aunt Phyllis is an influencer?

But… How?

L-O-L…

LOL. And Aunt Phyllis lives in Pasadena…

So… she's LOL Pasadena?

I don't know whether to laugh or cry.

When I get back to my room, the choice is easy:

I sob as I read the note Mary has left me:

I'm taking myself off the mission. You can send my things to Aunt Phyllis's place until I figure out what to do with my life.

Aunt Phyllis?...

LOL?

Mary doesn't know about that.

Truly, this is no laughing matter.

I call Mary's room. No answer.

I run to it. But no matter how hard I bang, no answer.

When I go back to my room, I call and ask the front desk to page her. "I'm sorry, ma'am, she's already checked out," I'm told.

I can't stop crying.

9

Cross-Channel

EACH INDIVIDUAL SOCIAL MEDIA NETWORK IS A MARKETING *channel. Taking the same message and having it seen (or heard) on every channel in your marketing plan is called a cross-channel strategy.*

You've also used this methodology with your family. For example, you've told them that dinner will be served at seven, so to show up at the table promptly, with hands washed.

And yet, sometimes, your point doesn't get through to one or more of your brood.

If your offer isn't resonating on social media, you either change the message, or the medium.

Guess what? You can do the same with your family!

One way to change the message: say it louder—with a bullhorn.

Or add a consequence. Perhaps lock them out of the house for being late.

Or in—say, the attic.

Either way, they'll get the message.

One saving grace: I don't hear a peep from Jack's room, so I guess he and the horny Hansley are playing pattycake somewhere else on this tremendous tugboat.

Then again, Hansley may be gagged in there. (Who knows? To each their own. No judgement, folks…)

I gnaw my fingers to the bone until finally I hear Jack's door close. A moment later, he's opened the one between our rooms.

He sees me pacing the floor. My raccoon eyes are a dead giveaway that something is terribly wrong.

He pulls me down on the bed with him. "What's happened?"

"Mary saw me seduce Grady. It freaked her out."

Jack frowns.

I hand him her note.

After he reads it, he curses under his breath and paces the floor.

"It gets worse," I tell him. "Trisha and Jeff are here too!"

"What?" Astonished, he turns to face me.

"You heard me. And they… they saw me. That is, they saw Miss Delish" —I turn away so that he can't see the tears in my eyes—"getting mauled in the hall by Grady."

"Oh, well, that's great." He sits down, pulling me with him. "What did you say to them?"

"Nothing. It's hard to speak when you've got someone's tongue down your throat."

"Why isn't Aunt Phyllis with them?"

"Oh, trust me—she's here, all right! Along with Lee and Janie and the rest of the soccer team—"

"*Lee Chiffray?*" Jack snorts. "So, that's what Hansley meant when she said she'd scored some very special VIP guests. I thought she meant a few actors or sports figures."

"If that's what Handsy Hansley considers pillow talk, then she's lucky she didn't mention that the surprise was Lee. The way you feel about him, it would have deflated your chance to impress her." I smirk as I shift my eyes to his crotch.

"In fact, she invited me—as well as Jonathan Morrow and Claudia Whitlock—to a dinner in the Captain's Quarters so that we could meet another investor who showed up today: a Ukrainian energy billionaire named Oleg Petrov. Emma's pulling up everything Acme can find on him right now."

"Oh…Well, then…"

"I accept your apology."

"None was offered," I huff.

"Then maybe you should consider ways you can make it up to me." Gently, he touches my cheek.

Even as I put my hand over his, I ask, "Are you forgetting that we're in the middle of a crisis? I haven't even told you the worst part!"

"Lee showing up here doesn't rate?" Jack snickers.

"Believe it or not, no." I roll my eyes.

"It must have been disappointing that your biggest fan didn't recognize you."

I shrug. "Frankly, I was relieved."

"Yeah, in hindsight, I could see why. He finds it hard enough to know you prefer me to him. The thought of you being mauled by a terrorist within feet of him would be too hard for him to take." His steely words belie his own feelings.

Mine too.

Lee is a different matter altogether. He's not married to me.

"We're just friends. He's accepted that," I insist.

Jack laughs raucously. "Yeah, keep telling yourself that."

It strikes me that we shouldn't come down so hard on Evan when we know exactly how he feels.

I sigh. "I still haven't told you the worst bit of news. Aunt Phyllis is LOL Pasadena."

Jack stares. Then he busts out laughing. "You're right! This just keeps getting better."

He pulls out his phone.

"Who are you calling?" I ask.

"Lee. The last place a former President of the United States should be is within shooting range of a group of terrorists who may be planning something to light up social media—and the skies over Washington DC. He needs to get his child—and our children too—out of here. By the way, if Mary wants to hitch a ride home on Lee's private jet, she's welcome to do so."

"You don't get it. After what she saw downstairs—of you with Hansley and me with Grady, she doesn't want to go home at all. You read the note."

"She's underage. She has to do what we say."

"She turns eighteen in a couple of days," I remind him.

He drops his head, perplexed—

But then he lifts it again to say: "Yeah, uh...Lee? Yes,

it's me, Jack. Am I right that you're on the Prince Charles ocean liner?... Yes, with Phyllis and the kids... No, she never got through to us to tell us that she's a FaceStaTweet sensation..." Jack looks up at the ceiling, as if he'll find his sanity there, but then sighs, as if he knows better. "Well, surprise, surprise, Donna and I are here as well—also on the Prince Charles!... Yeah, well, who knew the whole place would be swarming with social media types for some big shindig? We thought we'd have the whole place to ourselves. Hey, would you mind if we met with you? Privately, that is... Sure, we'll be right up." He clicks off.

"I don't know who will be more disappointed: the girls or Aunt Phyllis," I say.

"Who cares? As long as they're safe."

He's got a point.

A SECRET SERVICE AGENT OPENS THE DOOR TO THE Presidential Suite. After checking our ID and scanning us with a metal detector, she grudgingly lets us into Lee's suite.

In answer to Dominic's question, Jack's digs aren't the poshest in the joint.

Lee and Eve shake Jack's hand, then both kiss me on the cheek. "Your timing couldn't be better. Porter, Phyllis, and the girls are taking advantage of the reception downstairs so that I could take a breather," Lee explains. "Janie's security detail is there, as close as a second skin, so not to worry about the children's safety."

"We are worried, for good reason," Jack replies. "Lee,

Donna and I are here because Eagle and Snake is using the Facey awards as a terrorist reunion. In fact, it may be planning a major operation during the event."

The color drains from Eve's face. "Oh, dear! Then I should make arrangements for us to leave as soon as possible…" Her voice trails off when she hears what we all do: the engines are starting up.

The Prince Charles is leaving the dock.

Still, Eve gets up, phone in hand, and walks to the far side of the suite.

"Did you come just to bring Aunt Phyllis?" I ask.

"Well… frankly, yes," Lee explains. "After FaceSta-Tweet called to tell her she was a finalist, she realized there was no plane that would get her cross-country in time for tonight's event. The girls were on such a high about her newfound celebrity and since I have a private plane, I thought it was a great way to cap off their winning season and do a good deed for their beloved mascot. Eve called to purchase tickets. The event director—that Hansley woman —was pleased as punch to invite me as a VIP guest and to comp the whole team. Coach Middleton is here too, keeping them in line. Eve arranged for us to fly into BWI." He shrugs. "Little did I know that I walked them into an ambush."

"They'll be announcing Mr. Chiffray's attendance at the tournament tomorrow," Eve adds.

"My guess is that our adversaries already know he's here." Mario stands in the doorway.

Mary is with him.

I beckon her in, but she ignores me. When Mario walks in, she does too, but she stays at his side.

She's pale. Her face is pinched with worry.

"Did you bring reinforcements?" Jack asks.

"About five hundred yards from here in the bay, a frigate filled with Navy SEALs awaits my instructions to deploy to your ship," Mario informs us. "Worst case scenario: Section 706 of the Communications Law allows President Davenport to proclaim either a state of peril or a disaster or other national emergency and shut down Face-StaTweet. No Congressional approval of advance notice is needed."

"If Eagle and Snake get even a whiff that we're onto them, this place will be a bloodbath in no time," I warn.

"That's why DNI Branham prefers that Acme initiate silent extractions. Ideally, take them alive so that we can interrogate them about the big event planned for some time in the next twenty-four hours. Mary says it's possible, since you've gotten...er, *close*... to several targets." He smothers a smile.

Not Mary. She turns her head to stare at the wall.

"Four thus far," Jack replies. "Besides Lyle, we know for certain one other: a food influencer named Grady McDougall. Two other accounts received messages from Eagle and Snake, but we've yet to identify their owners. As we speak, Abu, Arnie, Evan, and Dominic are still roaming the reception, vetting other possible suspects."

"Were you able to persuade Lyle to give you any leads?" I ask.

Mario shakes his head. "He claims he'd not been in contact with anyone but his handler. Whoever it is runs not just him but the whole stable of FaceStaTweet influencers." Mario turns to Mary. "Considering what a great job you did at vetting him, shouldn't you be out there too?"

My daughter looks away. "I… I don't think I'm right for this assignment, sir. I'd prefer our previous arrangement. You know, shadowing you in the White House."

"I disagree. You've already proven to be much more useful here. You're a chip off the old block"—Nodding to Jack, he adds— "or two."

"I am nothing like them," Mary mutters.

Mario stares at her. "That's a shame, since they have all the traits that make them ideal for diplomatic intelligence. However, if you feel strongly about bowing out, feel free to stay in your cabin until Sunday morning, when we should dock again."

Mary starts to speak, but then thinks better of it. "I'm sorry, Mario. Of course, I'll finish my role in the mission. In fact I'll head down to the ballroom to see what I can do to facilitate Arnie's surveillance efforts."

His grimace softens. "I'd appreciate that."

He waits until she leaves, then says: "Mr. Chiffray, their boss and mine are up in arms about your unexpected appearance."

"I can see how it might throw a monkey wrench in the op. Shall we call them so that we can put our heads together on what they feel is the best course for collateral containment?"

He doesn't have to ask twice.

In a moment, both men are on speakerphone. Ryan barks, "It's a fine mess you've gotten us into, Sir."

"Sorry about that, Ryan. But you know, I get lonely on

that mountaintop, especially when the Craigs have left town." Lee winks at me.

And no, I don't mind that Jack bristles.

"Emma is also on the line. She has an update on the intel coming in from the Craigs' team members," Ryan explains.

"Good evening, everyone. First off, you should know that only two more influencers have had contact with the mysterious account that links the other suspects. They are the Lóng Twins who are dance contestants, and the lifestyle realtor, Sammy French."

I scroll through my FaceStaTweet account to put faces with these names.

"And all this time I thought that Sammy French was a man." I shake my head at the gorgeous woman whose latest post is a video of a sumptuous Manhattan penthouse apartment.

Jack looks over my shoulder and whistles. "Yet again, Dominic must rise to the occasion, poor guy."

I catch his eye, then nod in Mary's direction.

When he cringes, I know he got the message.

When I scroll to the Lóng Twins' account, what I see stops me cold. "My God! They're babies! Like, what, twelve, maybe?"

Jack frowns. "Could there have been a crossed signal during transmission?"

"That's a great question for Abu," Ryan points out. "I would imagine the twins are there with their parents."

"They are, and the parents, Hu and Ming, are their managers," Emma replies. "A dossier on the family is being put together as we speak. Thus far we know that the twins, Genghis and Guang, were born stateside. However, Ming and Hu immigrated from China. They were formerly ballroom dancers who escaped the mainland during a competition in British Columbia."

"Bingo," Jack murmurs. "I guess China's Ministry of State Security is putting the screws to them—perhaps through relatives they left behind."

"Or maybe their defection was part of their cover," I reason.

"Considering that they were within close proximity during the assassination of a Chinese scientist who'd defected here, I'd bet on the latter," Emma replies.

"In other words, take no chances that they're armed and dangerous." I say that for Mary's benefit.

"So, how can we stop them?" Mary asks.

"You'll get friendly with the kids," Jack says. "At the same time, I'll approach the parents with the suggestion that we discuss ways in which they should invest their children's sponsorship revenue. If they know you're a social media producer, they'll feel comfortable about walking away for a few moments."

She nods, satisfied. "When should we approach them?"

"I assume they'll have put the twins to bed by now, so that they'll be fresh for their competition. Let's cross paths with them at breakfast," Jack suggests.

"Donna, what were you able to get out of Grady?" Ryan asks.

"In keeping with your mandate to turn these operatives as opposed to exterminating them, I put him to sleep then searched his room. There were no weapons of any sort except the knives you'd expect a chef to carry. Emma, how did his computer check out?"

"Clean. Albeit he has a great recipe for Mulligatawny soup. And if your next question is whether I downloaded it for you, the answer is yes."

I laugh. "Thank you, girlfriend. How about Bake It or Fake It?"

"She's the real item."

"I'm glad. This has been a big break for her. Her last gig was short-ordering at a Waffle House in Marietta, Georgia." I shake my head at that plight. "I'll be honest, Ryan. Grady comes off like a chef, and nothing more. Could he be just an unknowing asset?"

"How would that explain his being at the wrong place at the right time? By that I mean the first-class compartment of an Air France flight carrying a French diplomat stateside, who ended up drugged while his briefcase was stolen. All he remembers was that the whole cabin was being wined and dined by Grady, who was demonstrating on how to give airline food a little gourmet flair."

"Grady is out like a light now, and he'll be groggy—and handcuffed—when he wakes up in the morning," I assure Ryan.

"You're an expert at disarming your targets at the right time and place," Ryan insists. "Sure, cosplay works."

Emma coughs—a hint to our boss that Mary is there.

Thank you, girlfriend.

But from Mary's wince, I know the hint comes too late.

Eve comes back into the room. "The girls are on their way back up."

"That's our cue to leave," Jack says.

"One last question. At what point can I get out of this gilded brig and play with my daughter and her friends?" Lee asks.

"I'm sure your security detail will appreciate you staying in this evening," Marcus points out. "Perhaps you can get a late start in the morning? What do you think, Ryan? Can the suspects be detained by lunch tomorrow?"

"We'll shoot for that, sir," Ryan declares.

By that, he means Jack and I have a lot on tomorrow's agenda.

"One more thing, Craigs," says Emma. "By triangulating one of Jack's unidentified transmissions with the flight clock, ComInt was able to determine that it was coming from the other side of a partition from where Jack was sitting at the time. We scrolled through the security footage until Mystery Man emerged. It was a bedroom where Hansley was napping."

Figures.

"Does that mean she was carrying two cells?" I ask.

"Our guess is yes," Emma concedes.

"As FaceStaTweet's liaison, she may be the lynchpin to the whole mission," Ryan reasons. "Jack, get a head start on it."

He means tonight.

Which means I'll be sleeping alone.

"By the way, Dominic cleared Sammy French," Emma tells us.

Jack grins. "What about Alana Partain?"

"She's in the clear," Emma snickers, "but Dominic is in hot water—literally. As in her cabin's hot tub."

"Now that she's been vetted, why doesn't he just get the hell out of dodge?" I ask.

"When he tried, she threw his tux overboard—along with everything else he was wearing. He's in the hot tub to keep warm. Abu is breaking into the cabin next to hers with an extra set of clothes. Afterward, he'll swing from her terrace to that one to make his escape."

"Tsk, tsk," I murmur. "How does he get himself into these predicaments?"

"It's the curse of being an International Man of Mystery with a FaceStaTweet account," Jack retorts.

"By the way, Arnie vetted Joe the Poser. He also vetted LOL Pasadena." Ryan guffaws. "I guess we now know why. Seriously, doesn't he recognize your aunt by now?"

"In his defense, she's been wearing some pretty silly get-ups," Emma explains.

"He wasn't able to vet Eric and Erica either," Ryan grumbles.

"Why not?" I ask.

"They didn't have their cells on them," Emma explains.

"That's certainly odd, considering that normally they post practically every minute of their day," I point out.

"Abu is on it," Ryan replies. "While Jody chats them up, he's going to break into their cabin and search it." He sighs heavily. "I don't like the thought of asking a civilian to play decoy, but with Dominic out of commission…Still, I give her kudos for going above and beyond the call of duty."

"Speaking of getting caught, we'd better skedaddle before the girls get back," Jack says. "Not to mention Aunt Phyllis."

Hearing her name, I groan. If she gets hurt in any crossfire, I'd never forgive myself.

I give Jack a kiss. "You head out with Mary. I need to check something with Lee." I turn to kiss Mary too but she's already walking toward the entrance of the suite.

I know a dodge when I see one.

"Listen Donna..." Lee grimaces. "One thing Branham isn't saying but that I know from experience is that if the terrorists do succeed in co-opting the event for a hostage takeover and blackmail, FaceStaTweet will go dark —permanently."

I chortle. "Maybe that's a good thing! Social media is too easy to disseminate lies, not to mention it's a waste of time. But I'll bring it up to Ryan, so we're prepared to grab what evidence we need before that happens." I force a smile on my lips before facing Lee. "Do me a favor. When Phyllis gets back to the room, will you tell her that a special fan would like her autograph? Give her this room number" —I jot it down for him— "but don't tell her it's me."

"Will do." He takes a long look at me. "You're worried she may get hurt."

"Yes. I could never forgive myself if she did."

"I'll send her down to you as soon as she gets back."

"Thanks, Lee."

He kisses me good night.

On the cheek.

As I walk out the door, I hear his wistful sigh.

10

Vanity Metric

Sometimes social media statistics may provide some positive indicator of performance, but don't provide valuable insights. This is known as a "vanity metric."

Take impressions, for example. As your followers scroll through their account feeds and see your post, it counts as an impression. But how many of them "like" it, let alone repost it — or leave a comment?

If you were to consider your life through its vanity metric, the number of people who see you — on the street walking your dog, in the grocery store, at your daughter's soccer game — may leave an impression on them. But when they come up say to hi, or pet your dog, or help you load your groceries into your car, or applaud your son's home run — well, now, that is true engagement.

It is what counts.

Be sure to engage with them too. It's the best kind of social — no media needed.

I'M PACING THE ROOM, WONDERING HOW TO TELL AUNT Phyllis that she needs to get the hell off this death ship when I hear a knock on the door. I look through the peep hole—

To find her standing there.

I fling open the door. Her surprise registers on her face. "Why, Miss Delish! I'm flattered that you—"

Before she can say anything else, I yank her into the room, closing the door behind us.

Then I pull off my wig. "Aunt Phyllis—It's me! Donna!"

After a doubletake, she whoops for joy. "You came! Oh, my sweet niece, I'm so happy you're here to share the biggest weekend of my life!" she exclaims. Aunt Phyllis's bear hug leaves me gasping.

I pat her back until she finally loosens her grip, then I move her to the settee. "Yeah, well about that—"

"No need to explain, I get it! You wanted to surprise me!" she pinches my cheek.

Ouch—

And I don't mean the pinch. I stammer, "In truth, I never—"

"Yeah, me neither! Who would have thought that I, in my dotage, would be a celebrity, a social media sensation" —Aunt Phyllis pulls out her cell. After a quick click, she scrolls until she finds what she's looking for—"with almost ninety million followers—"

"Wait! You've got that many?" I grab it out of her hand.

By golly, she does indeed!

Yikes.

"You betcha! I'm leading in my category—which is pretty amazing, considering how fierce the competition is! And the fact that I sort of waltzed into it—and at warp speed too! Go figure! Little ol' me—and I do mean 'old,' because let me tell you, while the rest of them are spring chickens, I am *anything* but—"

"Aunt Phyllis, please—you've got to listen to me! It's not safe for you to be here!"

"You're telling me!" She shakes her head in wonder. That Eric and Erica are pea-green with envy! If those eyes of theirs were daggers, I'd be dead already—"

"That's what I'm trying to tell you! Aunt Phyllis, I'm worried that you'll be a target—"

She nods adamantly. "And don't I know it! You know those Lóng Twins? Why, I caught one of them spitting into my mug of Metamucil! I boxed her ears solidly. I thought that mama of hers was going to kill me! I just hope my little lecture scared the Bejeezus out of her. I told her: 'Wait until you are my age, missy, and you need a little sumthin'-sumthin' to push things through that funhouse we call a colon—"

I slap my hand over her mouth. "That's my point! The Lóngs *are* killers!"

Phyllis's eyes open wide. When I pull my hand away from her mouth, I see that her jaw has dropped. "What do you mean?"

"A terrorist organization communicates with their soldiers of fortune via FaceStaTweet. Ironically, these killers are some of the social network's highest-ranking influencers. Acme doesn't know exactly what will happen, but we do know that something bad will take place during tomorrow evening's two-hour tournament unless we can stop it. To make things worse, the Prince Charles has sailed from the dock. As far as the NSA is concerned, FaceSta-Tweet's two hundred guests are being held hostage in the middle of Chesapeake Bay—*with a former president onboard.* That's a pretty big notch on any terrorist's belt."

Aunt Phyllis's eyes tear up. And yet, she's laughing. "I guess what you're trying to tell me is that you weren't really here for me, *per se.*"

Now I'm wiping away tears too—of both joy and sorrow. "You know I love you. Truly, Aunt Phyllis, under normal circumstances, nothing would have stopped me from being at your side and cheering you on—*absolutely nothing!*"

A sad smile tries to make it to the corners of Aunt Phyllis's mouth but fails miserably. "I know you would, my dear sweet Donna." She shrugs. "I missed out on *Hullabaloo*! I missed out on *Soul Train*! And, okay, granted, I got thrown out of *American Bandstand*." She rolls her eyes. "I was too much of a dirty dancer for Mr. Dick Clark. Darn it, this is my one shot at fame!" She shrugs. "What are the chances you'll round up the bad guys before the tournament begins?"

"Right now, Jack and I are working undercover to figure out who they are, and we're rounding them up. Thus far, we've arrested one. Two, possibly three others will be in handcuffs by tomorrow morning—including the parents of the Lóng Twins. Eric and Erica are still suspects. They'll be vetted by tomorrow."

"Goodness, I hope one of the terrorists isn't Joe the

Poser! He's a real doll. And those moves! That kid can cut a rug."

"No problem there. He's been vetted and cleared."

"Well, now, that's good to know since he's meeting me back at my cabin in about five minutes. He wants to choreograph a dance that he feels will be perfect for me." She thinks for a moment. "I'll tell you who you should have your eyes on. He's in my category: the Sleek Sikh. He's all hands, no feet. How he got to the finals is beyond me! He must have CGI'ed his moves. As for his beatboxing, I swear it's a voiceover. Frankly, his cadence is too much like Mark Martin's. Talk about suspicious—"

"Not to worry, Aunt Phyllis. He's one of our mission team: Abu Nagashahi. Also undercover are Arnie, Dominic"—I hesitate, but then add, "and Mary and Evan."

She slaps her hand to her forehead. "Acme must have great stylists on staff! I didn't recognize any of you! Ha! Remind me to stop at your office for a makeover before I go out on the town with Porter." Her eyes open wide. "I've just realized something. With the Sleek Sikh and the Lóng Twins out of the way, you've eliminated two contestants in my category. Even if Eric and Erica end up with a clean bill of health, I've got a one-in-three chance of winning. I'll make a deal with you: I'll do my posts from in my cabin up until showtime. By then, you should have taken care of business."

I grimace. "Pinky square? No sneaking out?"

"Not if my life depends on it," she vows.

"It does."

She winces at the gravity in my voice. "Then you have my answer."

We shake on it. "I'll walk you to your door," I suggest. "But first, let me put this wig back on and grab my handcuffs."

"Hey, no need for any rough stuff! I promised you I'd stay in my cabin until the coast is clear, and I meant it."

"Trust me, they're not for you."

"Ah—I get it!" Aunt Phyllis gives me a wink. "You want to surprise Jack with some rough and tumble, eh?" She sighs. "Ah, young love!"

As promised, Joe the Poser is waiting for Aunt Phyllis. A twenty-something with an impish smile, I can tell he's smitten with my aunt.

She introduces me, but almost slips up by calling me "Miss Do…I mean, Miss *Delish*."

Joe bows with a flourish.

After we enter her cabin, he hands her the dress bag he's carrying over his shoulder. "This little cocktail gown has a ton of shake and shimmy built into it," he explains.

When he unzips it, we see what he means: it boasts metallic sequins from shoulder to thigh.

Aunt Phyllis's eyes sparkle. "It's perfect! I'll really shine in this little number."

"I'm glad you love it," he gushes. "Well, we better get to work. You've got a whole new choreography to learn: all the retro stuff you love—the Mash Potato, the Swim, The Watutsi—but with some awesome club moves that bring them home in a whole new way."

I don't have the heart to tell them that if Acme doesn't

succeed in its mission, FaceStaTweet may be taken down permanently.

I leave them to do their thing.

As I'd hoped, Grady is still cutting zee's. I take the cuffs and secure his hands to the headboard. With a couple of his belts, his legs are secured to the bed's footboard. Being spread-eagled leaves one with little modesty. I remedy that by placing a pillow over his groin.

And a sock in his mouth, to stifle his screams.

I code DO NOT DISTURB on his cabin phone. I'd hoped to turn off his cell, but I can't find it.

Odd.

Before leaving, I also put the DO NOT DISTURB sign on his doorknob in case his entourage comes looking for him.

11

Traffic

In SM terms, "traffic" indicates the number of users who click onto a website page.

What you want to be able to say is "Traffic is great."

In S&M parlance, "traffic" is a (small) head count of naughty clients on any given week.

Again: "Traffic is great" says it all.

In your real life, traffic is what you and thousands of others sit in while hoping to run your errands, get to work, or take your family to or from their appointed destinations in a timely fashion.

As for hearing the words "traffic is great…"

Dream on.

WHEN I GET BACK TO MY CABIN, I CHANGE INTO MY JAMMIES: in this case, a peignoir, and its matching robe: something Miss Delish would wear. I don't have to stay in character, but since I share Miss Delish's wardrobe—and hers is vintage couture—then why not?

Maybe Aunt Phyllis is right. A little costume play may relieve the tension—mine and Jack's. And Miss Delish's wardrobe is a turn-on, with or without the handcuffs.

I put my ear to the door adjoining Jack's. To my dismay, he has company after all:

I hear the murmur of conversation. A throaty laugh. The creak of the bed. The rustle of sheets.

A steady *thump... thump… thump…*

He must be "interrogating" Hansley.

Getting up close—and very personal—with our targets is a necessary evil of our jobs.

I hate it.

Ecstatic groans.

Then silence.

For much too long…

I grab the glass again and put it up against the wall—

Bad timing, since at exactly that moment Hansley lets loose with an ear-piercing scream.

Ah, good. Finally, he's torturing her.

Slaps and punches come next. Then, a few slams that shake the wall between us.

She certainly is putting up quite a fight…

Then I hear Jack's deck door slide open—

And Hansley's scream—

Before a loud splash.

I run out onto my deck.

Hansley has fallen face down into the bay. Her gauzy skirt floats through the water, revealing her nakedness beneath it. A trail of blood, coming from the bullet hole that pierced her back directly behind her heart, clouds the water.

Shite! We're supposed to interrogate, not exterminate—unless it's necessary. Did she attack Jack when he confronted her with what we know?

I turn but not quick enough before the door to his deck shuts on a pitch-dark bedroom—

I open our adjoining door—

There is a groan…

Jack lays on the floor, unconscious.

I hear footsteps. Someone is in the living room.

When in honeypot mode, Jack usually hides a gun between the mattress and the headboard. I grab it. Silently, cautiously, I inch my way out of the bedroom—

To find the cabin's front door is shutting with a click.

Who went out the door?

I'm torn between chasing after my husband's attacker and administering to the man I love.

I run to Jack.

No blood, thank God. A few slaps on his cheeks aren't bringing him back to me, so I open a bottle of water and splash his face with its contents.

He gasps before coming to. Jack stares at me then rises to his feet, but he stumbles because he's still dizzy. He looks around. "Where is…"

"Hansley is floating in the bay." I point toward the deck's sliding door. "She was shot in the back at close range. Her shooter shoved her over your balcony."

"Aw, hell!" Jack buries his head in his hands. "She was just about to tell me who's running the terrorists!" He starts for the front door and throws it open, but stops short, staring down the hall one way, then another. Dismayed, he comes back into the suite. With a sigh, he drops onto the bed.

Hansley's lacy thong lies on the floor. I pick it up and hand it to him. "So...I take it that you convinced her to talk?"

"After we...well, you know...yes, we'd begun a heart-to-heart." Jack shrugs. "But before it got further than a little close cuddling, I told her enough to convince her that she was in trouble; to come clean, or else she'd be tried as an accomplice. She admitted that Eagle and Snake is blackmailing her. Besides giving their operatives free rein of the event, she was supposed to seduce FaceStaTweet's investors so that we'd be blackmailed by the terrorists. They communicate with her through a cell that is not registered to her. She did confirm what we'd already suspected: that the Lóngs are dirty. Lyle too, as well as Eric and Erica, although I think they too have an anonymous cell phone, which is why we couldn't pick up their signal on the plane. Speaking of the plane, she said that there was another terrorist on it. She was about to tell me who when someone picked me up from behind and heaved me against the wall. We were in the bedroom when he slipped into my suite. Before I could turn around and hit back, I was slammed into another wall. I was knocked out cold." He rubs the bump on his head.

"What did Hansley say about Grady?"

Jack sighs. "I hadn't gotten around to asking her about him."

"Could he have been the other terrorist she mentioned who was on the plane?"

"It's plausible. But I got the feeling that it was someone else." He rubs his temples, as if doing so will help him remember something.

"That's okay. At least we know Grady didn't kill her. He's tied down in his bed. When he comes to, I'll enjoy getting the truth out of him." I touch the blackening bruise on Jack's temple.

He winces.

"Let me get some ice on that," I insist. After taking a few cubes from the ice bucket, I head to the bathroom for a hand towel.

When I return, he's anxiously scanning the room.

"What's wrong?" I ask.

"Her clutch purse was there, on the dresser. Now it's gone."

"Your assailant probably took it."

Jack snickers. "I'm sure it was live-streaming our tryst for their blackmail purposes."

"They got that—and, unfortunately, your attempt to turn her." I sigh. "Your cover is blown. And for all we know, they may be on their way now to finish the job—and to pin her death on you." I hand him his icepack. "Grab your things. You're now rooming with me."

"I thought you'd never ask." He attempts a chuckle, but even smiling gives him a pain in his neck.

EVEN BEFORE WE'VE SHUT THE ADJOINING DOOR AND LOCKED it, Jack's cell rings with the opening stanza from *Jaws*.

"Speak of the devil," he mutters. "Ryan, we were just going to call you…*What?…*"

There's a knock on my door.

I freeze, but Jack beckons me to open it. When I peek through the keyhole, I see why:

Mary, Evan, Dominic, and Mario are standing outside. Abu and Arnie, still sporting their undercover personas, are right behind them. They are pushing a food cart laden with delicious desserts.

I open the door. "An impromptu party? Sure, why not?"

They traipse in just in time to hear Jack explain: "—murdered and thrown overboard, off my cabin deck."

In unison, Mary and Evan's faces go pale. Their eyes shift to each other.

Once my door is closed, Arnie and Abu pull out bags from beneath the food carts which contain HazMat suits, masks, goggles, gloves, shoe covers, ultra-violet lights, and Acme's failsafe concoction for wiping away anything that would indicate Hansley had been in Jack's suite.

As they suit up, Jack beckons Mario, Evan, Dominic, and Mary to the phone. "…Yes, they're here now…. Okay, I'll put you on speaker."

"Emma is on too," Ryan declares. "ComInt picked up the attack through your ear buds. But because you didn't see your attacker, unfortunately, neither could we. In preparation that Hansley's body is spotted in the next couple of hours and the ship's security team comes knocking on Jack's door, Abu and Arnie will deep-clean Jack's quarters of any trace of her. And frankly, I've got to hand it to Arnie for coming up with a great way to hide you in plain sight."

Jack grimaces. "Oh yeah? Let me guess. Do I spend the rest of the mission dressed in a bunny suit?"

"Close, but not as funny, old boy. In fact, you'll be much handsomer." He puts the valise in his hand on the table, then opens it.

Inside is a mask of Dominic's face.

Jack stares down at it. "Ryan… You're kidding, right?"

"Frankly, I think it's brilliant," Ryan proclaims. "But I feel your pain. The thought of two Dominic Flemings does boggle the mind."

"It doesn't do much for the libido either," I mutter. "Mine, anyway."

"Ditto," Jack grumbles.

"It could have been worse," Ryan warns. "Arnie was going to make a mask of his own face."

The look of horror on Jack's face is priceless. Then again, I'm sure mine mirrors it.

"What about Dominic's fans?" Jack asks. "I can't be incognito if I have to fight them off."

"I doubt seriously anyone will mistake you for the real deal," Dominic sniffs. To make his point, he turns to my full-length mirror. Staring at himself, he adds: "As badly as you wish it to be, you must face facts, old boy. I mean, just look at me! I'm taller, with an Olympian's physique, and always fashionably dressed in bespoke attire. Not to mention that my perfect posture is why I'm continually mistaken for a Royal." Dominic smiles supremely. "And with your dull, mousy brown hair, at the very most, someone may consider you a fifth cousin twice removed—

to, say, the Ozarks." He tosses Jack the mask. "Care to try it on for size?"

Jack mutters, "I'm sure my head is fat enough."

Still, he turns to the mirror. With a few nips and tucks, the mask is in place.

He looks over at me. "Well…what do you think?"

Gritting my teeth, I murmur, "It'll do…in a pinch."

NOT.

Brunette Dominic: not so bad looking.

Two Dominics: two too many.

"Then, it's settled," Ryan declares. "By the way, Evan bought you jeans, a few tee-shirts and a windbreaker to complete the disguise of the anti-Dominic."

"In other words, nothing I'd be caught dead in," Dominic assures Jack. "As the saying goes, clothes make the man."

"That is *so* not true," I respond. "Otherwise, every man in a tux would be viewed as a vaingloriously pompous ass—"

"Enough bickering, folks," Ryan warns. "Emma needs to bring you up to speed on a very important matter."

A moment of silence is enough for Ryan to know he's been heard.

"As you know, ComInt has been negotiating with the mystery account as Randy and Candy Murphy," Emma begins. "The MSS have agreed to a price that has Eagle and Snake salivating to get its hands on the China Lake Basin Naval Air Station intel that it thinks is in Candy and Randy Murphy's possession," Emma reminds us. "This is our chance to release the Trojan on the Chinese. We'll be resurrecting them with latex masks that are exact duplicates of their faces, as well as the voice-altering cell phone app courtesy of DARPA that you used when bringing the treasonous tech entrepreneur, Milo Cathcart, back to life."

"Great," I say. "When do Jack and I meet with the Wizard behind the curtain?"

"The handoff happens tomorrow morning, at eleven." —Ryan pauses, then adds—"But it will be Mary and Evan impersonating the Murphys."

"Wait...*what?*" Jack and I exclaim. Our eyes go to our daughter and her boyfriend.

Seeing the horror in my face, Mary says, "Mom, Evan and I are willing to do it."

"Over my dead body—or worse, yours or Evan's." Jack points toward my deck door. "Floating not twenty feet away from us is a dead woman who will soon be shark chum!"

I glare at Mario. "I'll bet this was your idea."

Silently, his eyes slide to Mary.

He wants *her to* cover for *him?* The nerve!

As I belt him in the gut, Mario grunts and doubles over. In time, he gasps, "Wrong! It was their idea. They're the right build—not to mention the right age."

"Another reason Mary isn't doing your dirty work. She's not yet eighteen."

"Mom...you forget. I was eighteen as of midnight tonight."

Oh, hell! I lost track of time—and forgot my daughter's birthday!

What the hell is wrong with me?

I am a terrible, terrible mom...

Yes, my job is to save the world. But first and foremost,

keeping her safe—along with her brother and sister—is my top priority.

Which is why I say, very firmly, "Mary please…it's…it's too dangerous!"

"Mom, please! They make the money transfer into a crypto account controlled by Acme, and then we hand over the SD card. What could be simpler?"

I look down at my feet so that Mary doesn't see my tears. "It is never simple. Too many things can go wrong. All it takes is one tiny mistake and we lose you or Evan." I take her hand. "If something happened to him, could you forgive yourself?" My gaze moves to him. "What if Mary got hurt—or worse, killed? How would you feel?"

They look at each other. The anger and anxiety that has gnawed at them this past week is now replaced with loving resolve. "Awful," Evan admits. "But we'd feel worse if we didn't do our bit to finish the mission you started. And we know that, together, we'll have each other's backs, just like Jack has yours and you have his."

Mary smiles up at him. "Thank you, partner. I feel exactly the same way."

"Always," Evan declares fervently, "And forever."

The look in Mary's eyes says she wishes she could kiss him, right then and there.

"Do you really think that Eagle and Snake is going to let Randy and Candy waltz off into the sunset, after having blackmailed it for an astronomically higher recovery fee?"

"We'll have eyes and ears on them at all times," Ryan reminds me.

"The beauty of this intricate charade is that the exchange takes place on the busiest place on the boat: the pool deck," Dominic pipes up. "I've reserved the cabana next to the one where it will happen. The exact moment that our young colleagues leave the courier's cabana, a few friends and I shall intercept the target so that Mary and Evan cannot be followed. They'll duck into my cabana, peel off their masks, step out of their clothes. Beneath it, they'll be wearing new duds."

"What if the courier has a goon squad with shoot-to-kill orders?" Jack asks.

"They won't find them amidst my hard-partying motley crew of the young and the beautiful who shall also be dressed exactly the same, in my new Dominic Fleming-label signature attire: gold lamé bikinis, sun hats, sunglasses, six-inch heels for the damsels, and tux jackets sans shirts, with jeans, and straw hats for the gents."

"Great, Ryan. At the same time, I assume you'll allow Donna and me to shadow them." Coming from Jack, it's not a question. It's a forgone conclusion.

"Yes…under one condition," Ryan replies. "That the drop isn't happening at the same time you're intercepting the Lóngs or Eric and Erica. Remember, until they're on ice, everyone on this boat is their hostage—including Evan and Mary."

"If the Lóngs still have ties with China's MSS, I would imagine they are the couriers," I say.

"And now that my cover is blown with Eagle and Snake, I can't use the ploy of a business breakfast with them," Jack points out. We'll have to get on the Lóngs's dance cards as soon as possible—like, tonight."

"We'll then tackle Eric and Erica," I vow.

"It will certainly be *a Lóng* night for the Craigs—pun intended," Mario declares.

If looks could kill, he'd be incinerated right then and there, by our glares.

"You'll find the Lóngs's stateroom two doors down from LOL Pasadena's—I mean, Aunt Phyllis's," Emma says. "They have a three-bedroom suite. The kids go to bed early. The adults are asleep by midnight."

"So we still have a couple of hours before we make our move," I reply.

"You'll get in with a keycard that has been coded for entry to their suite," Emma explains. "You'll find it in Arnie's bag, there beside you, along with some gas masks. We'll be knocking them out with a sleeping gas through the vents. Craigs, you'll have ComInt's eyes and ears until you're inside. Wait for my signal so that I can loop an empty hall for the security detail. By the way, I've recoded Jack's room key and it's now reserved under a different name on the door—one Eagle and Snake won't be looking for."

"Gotcha," Jack says. "How about Eric and Erica?"

"They have the room directly across the hall from Aunt Phyllis," Emma replies.

"Then we're all set," Jack says.

"How did it go with Aunt Phyllis?" Mary asks.

"She was happy to see me, but naturally she's disappointed about why we're here. She sees the Faceys as her last shot to fame and fortune and here we are, yanking the rug out from under her."

"Better than being thrown overboard," Ryan declares.

I kiss Mary's forehead, and then Evan's cheek. "Tomorrow is a big day. Try to get some rest."

They nod as they follow the others out the door.

I can tell that they're anxious. As they should be. It will keep them on their guard.

I don't want to point out that, if anything goes wrong, my daughter may not live to see her nineteenth birthday.

NOW THAT WE'RE ALONE, JACK EASES ONTO THE COUCH. I SIT beside him. Scanning his bruises, I don't like what I see. They are going from blue to bluer.

When I touch one on his bicep, he winces.

"Shall I kiss it and make it better?" I ask.

His answer: a hungry kiss.

But when I lean into it, he grunts from his pain.

"I've got the right medicine for that," I whisper. "Let me start a warm bath...with bubbles."

"Only if you'll join me."

"Of course I will..." I hesitate.

"What's the matter?" Jack asks.

"Well... Um..." How do I put this delicately? Ah hell— just go for it: "How about taking off that mask now?"

"Jeez! I forgot what—I mean, who, I look like!" Jack walks to the mirror—

And tugs.

Nothing.

He tugs again.

It won't peel off.

Now he's clawing at it. "The harder I pull, the tighter this damn thing gets!"

"Okay, okay—don't panic!" I'm beside him in a flash. I try picking at it with my nail, right under his chin.

He jerks away guffawing. "That tickles. Only it's not funny."

"Tell me about it." I shudder.

"Let's just forget about it," Jack mutters glumly.

"No! We're not going to let Dominic—or his face—get the better of us." To prove that I mean business: I shed my robe.

The peignoir drops to the floor.

As I walk to the bathroom, I feel Jack's eyes on me.

Knowing that he's watching my every move, I reach up on my toes to the shelf holding the jar of sweet pink bubble bath powder. My generous breast, in profile, elicits a longing sigh from my husband.

I know Jack watches the curve of my hip as I bend over to turn the hot and cold handles. By the time I've put a heaping handful of powder in the roiling water, Jack is behind me.

He lifts me into the tub.

Together, we drop into the water.

As he slips under me, I drop onto my knees, straddling him.

He enters me.

As we find our rhythm, our bodies slap against each other, churning the steaming water into sweet-smelling foaming waves. As an urgent passion rises in me, I move both hands against the cold porcelain tub to steady myself.

Can Jack hear my gasps, or are they drowned out by his moans coupled with his syncopated thrusts?

When I peak, he clasps me tightly against his chest. Our bodies curl into the warm fizzy water. As the steam rises beyond the cool air above us, I hear his whisper, "I love you with all my heart."

No words were ever sweeter.

INSISTENT POUNDING ON A DOOR IS INCONVENIENT ANY TIME, but especially when you're curled up in a bathtub with the man you love.

Grumbling, I step out of the tub, grab a robe, and wrap it around myself. I also wrap a towel around my head since I don't have time to slap on Miss Delish's wig.

The peephole exaggerates the size of the security officer staring back at me.

I crack open the door. "I'm, um…in the middle of a bath."

"Sorry to disturb you, but there was an incident in the next cabin. Did you hear anything?" Bug-Eye has another officer with him.

"Nope. Threw a little party myself, so if anyone else had a hullaballoo, I wouldn't have known about it."

"We're talking murder. Someone went overboard." He nudges into my cabin. "Mind if we take a look around?"

"Sure…but there's not much to see here." I allow the loose belt of my robe to prove me wrong.

It's human nature to stare into the sun. A woman's breasts have the same effect on men.

Go figure.

Finally Bug Eye peels his eyes away, then taps Second Guy as a warning to do the same. "Sorry, but…orders," he mutters.

I sashay toward the bathroom. "Well, then excuse me while I powder my nose."

Before I can close the door, Bug Eye is on my heels and looking over my shoulder—

At my tub.

All he sees is a mound of bubbles.

"Like I said, you disturbed me." As I drop a shoulder, my breast plays peek-a-boo with him again, leaving him mesmerized.

Finally, I snap my fingers in his face. "Show's over. Or should I call head of security?"

Grudgingly he nods.

As they lumber out, I lock the door behind them—

And then run back into the bathroom to give Jack the all-clear.

He leaps up from the mountain of bubbles, gasping.

Or, to my eyes, Dominic does.

Because I'd forgotten about Jack's masquerade, I hold my hand over my mouth to keep from screaming.

Or gagging.

By the time I've collected myself enough to smile, Jack has caught his breath.

He sighs. "Well, at least we know my new face is waterproof."

What a shame, I think. But I don't say it.

He deserves a kiss for being such a great sport.

I manage it without gagging. Or laughing.

12

Social Media Crisis

IF SOMEONE LEAVES A BAD REVIEW ON YOUR POST, PLEASE don't build this up in your mind as a social media crisis.

If you get fewer hearts or likes to a post, do not despair. Again, no biggy!

Trolls will troll, friends will ghost, ghosts will post—

It's all part of the social media game. No crisis here, folks, so keep it moving.

Now, if someone breaks into your account and begins posting stuff that you'd never say or do, that is indeed a media crisis!

Solution: Close the account.

"THE HALL MONITOR IS ON BREAK, AND SANDMAN IS IN THE building." This is Emma's way of telling us that the ship's SecCam is on a loop, and the Lóngs have been knocked out cold. Now that the sleeping gas has done its trick, we've got the all-clear to enter without getting woozy ourselves.

"We're on our way," Jack replies.

In case we cross paths with any of Dominic's gawking fans, Jack has on glasses, a bushy mustache, and a baseball cap sporting the Arkansas Razerbacks' logo. As for me, I'm not dressed in any of my Miss Delish wardrobe. Instead, I'm wearing jeans, a casual top, and a dark jacket. I also wear a baseball cap—one which Jeff gave me on my last birthday. It has a San Francisco Giants logo.

In other words, we're just two FaceStaTweet fans walking down a hall, looking to score autographs from our favorite social media influencers.

We hope we'll only need the zip ties to subdue them. But just in case, we've come armed with stun guns, and if things get out of hand: our Sig Sauer P229s are holstered inside our waistbands at the appendix.

Using our duplicated hotel room card, we tip-toe into the Lóngs's suite. The door to the children's bedroom is shut, whereas the door to their parent's room is wide open.

Their mother, book in hand, sits up in bed. However, my guess is that the sleeping gas had nothing to do with the fact that it has fallen onto her lap. The bullet hole in her forehead was the culprit.

The shot that took her husband out was direct to his heart. He must have been walking out of the bathroom because the force of the shot threw him back against the vanity.

The water is still running.

Outside the porthole window, we hear sobs.

We reach across the bathtub to look outside.

The boy, Genghis, is comforting his sister, Guang, who

is sobbing. So that I don't call attention to us, Jack puts a finger to his lips and points to something the boy holds:

It's the smallest Springfield on the market—the XDe—but it's just as deadly as any other nine-millimeter semi-automatic pistol.

The proof is next to us.

So, why did he murder his parents?

Why didn't the gas incapacitate the children? Was it because they went outside after the assassinations?

After nudging me back inside and into the master suite, Jack whispers: "He's old enough to know what he's done. And considering the accuracy of his shots, to save his skin—*and hers*—he won't be afraid to do it again. There are two ways onto the suite's terrace: from this room, and the living room. I say we split up. You cover this room, and I'll approach from the living room. That way, we flank them."

I nod.

Jack takes off.

I move back to the terrace door, crouching low, so that they don't see me.

Suddenly, Genghis shoves his sister to the floor and raises his gun in the direction of the living room.

I scream, *"Genghis—NO!"*

He swings the gun in my direction—

But when I toss my cap in his face, he's distracted enough that he pauses, confused—

Giving Jack the time he needs to wrench the gun from the boy's hand.

Genghis is all over Jack. His kick hits its target: Jack's solar plexus. When he falls against the rail, both children jump on him, shoving and biting. Their goal is to regain the advantage that the gun gave them.

The stun gun's shock—first to Genghis, then to Guang, leaves them paralyzed on the deck floor.

Jack turns in time to vomit over the deck's rail.

When I reach him, he's down to dry heaves. In time, he gasps, "The kid packs quite a kick."

"He was going to shoot you! But I just couldn't shoot a child. And I was too far away to stun him, so I thought distracting him would give you enough time—"

"Donna, babe, it's okay! You did the right thing."

I shiver in Jack's arms. "Before they come to, we should bind their hands…just in case."

He nods, but I can tell he doesn't like that idea any more than me. They are still kids, after all.

Trained to be killers.

Is that what I'm doing to Mary, training her to be a killer, like me?

And like me, she believes she can make a difference.

But how far will she go in the service of our country? Would she take a life?

She may have to—perhaps to save her own.

Jack secures Genghis while I tie up Guang. Their moans reflect their fear as to who we are and what we will do with them. They are light enough to heave over the rail, to perish in the dark currents of Chesapeake Bay.

The girl holds something in the palm of her hand: a cell phone. As I pry it away from her, fear widens her eyes.

She was texting someone:

Our parents are nuts. They plan to kill everyone here on the ship, on orders from some terrorist group. Apparently, they still work for China's secret service. They want to go back as heroes—and take us with them! They are going to blow everything we've worked so hard for! The people who now love us will hate us! You say you knew people who can stop them. Please, save me and my brother before

The missive stops there. Genghis's rampage took place before she had a chance to send it.

I recognize the phone number: it belongs to Jody Keleske.

I pull my cell from my pocket and call Jody. Her voice, husky with sleep, murmurs, "Yes, hello?"

"It's Donna. I'm in the Lóngs's cabin: 713. With the twins. Can you join us?"

"Yes! Of course! But..." After a pause: "I'm with Dominic. Should I bring him?"

Ha!...

I guess she's forgiven him his indiscretions for flag and country.

I know from experience it's not easy to do.

"Sure, the more the merrier," I say. "Oh!... and warn him that Jack is here too."

Otherwise Dominic will assume he's looking in a mirror.

If we don't find a way to peel that mask off after this mission, I'll have to learn to make love blindfolded...

Hmmm. Well, that's one way to spice things up.

By the time Jody and Dominic get here, we've confiscated all weapons in the Lóngs's suite, and the twins are recovered from their stun gun shocks.

Jody does a doubletake when she sees Dominic's face but hears Jack's voice emerging from it. And yet, she keeps mum. I've got to give her credit: the cough that covers her giggle is realistic enough.

As for the awe and anguish over the adult Lóngs's plans: not so much.

Genghis is particularly livid. "What did they think, that we'd jump at a chance to go to a country where your every move is watched? That we'd love becoming what they were—puppets who jump through hoops, who do horrible things?"

"They weren't parents. They were drill sergeants." Guang's lower lip trembles as she speaks. "From the very beginning, everything in our lives was scheduled or programed: schooling, dancing, martial arts, target practice—"

"And if we begged for a day off, if we questioned anything—" Genghis scowls at the thought.

"They'd beat us." Guang drops her head, ashamed.

"Or starve us," Genghis mutters.

"My brother was starved for three days, just because he wouldn't shoot our dog." Tears glisten in Guang's eyes. "It was the only pet they allowed us—"

Genghis nods. "A puppy. It peed on the floor."

"Ming called it disgusting," Guang adds.

"You called your mother by her first name?" I ask.

Genghis snorts. "She wasn't our mother. Nor was Hu our father. If we annoyed them, they called me Test Tube One, and Guang was Test Tube Two." He takes his sister's hand. "Remember when that boy at one of the dance competitions flirted with you?"

Guang recoils. In time, she nods. "Hu got to him in the men's room. Took a knife to his throat and threatened to cut his hamstring so that he'd never walk again, let alone dance." She shrugs. "It's why we don't have friends."

"They said we could trust no one. Only them. They said we'd soon be… well…" Genghis turns red. "Ripe for plucking." He gives his sister a sidelong glance. "You know, Ming boasted that on my thirteenth birthday she would show me how to be a man."

Guang shivers. "Hu… said soon I would be a woman. And that…that he would be my first."

Her brother glowers. "I'm glad I shot them."

Guang throws her arms around him, holding him tight.

"You did so in self-defense," I acknowledge.

Genghis' relief shows itself in the tears flowing down his cheeks. He now knows that his nightmare is over.

When Jack puts his hand on the boy's shoulder, he doesn't flinch. Instead, he leans into it. "How did you know to reach out to Jody?" Jack asks.

Both kids gaze up at Jody. "Are you kidding? In the influencer world, Jody is epic!" Genghis exclaims.

"We'd be honored to work with her!" Shyly, Guang looks up at Jody. "She's known to take her clients to the next level, or three. Like, I heard you counseled Sweet Meat on how to double his contract with the barbecue company that is his sponsor."

"And that gamer dude who had a chance to work with you but stupidly turned you down—what's his name again? Oh yeah, *Cheever*." Genghis guffaws. "He thinks it's all his own doing. What an idiot!"

"Guang, did Hu and Ming tell you specifically what was to happen today, and when?"

The twins shrug. "We'd overheard them saying that something big was to go down during the tournament. They told us that when the time came, they'd keep us safe because too much time and money had been invested in us," Guang explains.

"While on the Prince Charles, did they take private meetings with anyone?" Jack asks.

"They'd just gotten back from one, but we don't know where it took place, or with whom." Genghis replies. "When we're not on display to fans, they lock us in our rooms. But whatever was said there got them excited about going back to China."

"Did they mention rendezvousing with anyone tomorrow prior to the tournament?" I ask. I'm thinking of Mary and Evan. If they were to meet with Hu and Ming, then the exchange won't be happening. Mario will be disappointed, but I couldn't care less about that. Pulling off the extortion of a terrorist group isn't something you learn in Spycraft 101. More like a master class.

Few graduate with the honor of living to a ripe old age.

"Our schedule for today is dance practice in the morning," Guang explains. "Then we're to have lunch with potential sponsors. The afternoon is supposed to be devoted to our fans: signing autographs, taking selfies, teaching a few VIP fans a new dance. You know, that sort of thing,"

Jack's question: "And both of them were to stay at your side the whole time?"

"Up until an hour ago, one or both of them never let us out of their sight," she insists.

"Why would they? We were their golden ticket, their pot of gold at the end of the rainbow," Genghis mutters. "They control the money. We're just…normal kids!"

And, until now, they were the Lóngs's cover.

Without them, Hu and Ming couldn't receive their coded extermination orders.

Speaking of which:

"Did Ming and Hu do all of your producing and posting?"

The twins nod. "Every word that came out of our mouths was scripted, as was every dance move."

Guang gets up and walks into the master bedroom. When she returns, she's holding a notebook. She hands it to us.

Specific phrases, noted by date and time, fill its lined pages. "There are seven more of these," she explains. "One for every year since we first went on social media."

The Lóngs kept an eight-year archive of their missions? Wow, Emma's team will have a field day deciphering it!

"Just out of curiosity, did you ever say or do something that wasn't scripted?" Jack asks.

The twins exchange shamed looks. Reluctantly, Genghis gets up to peel off his tee shirt.

His back has a burn mark. It looks as if it was made by a cigar.

I hold back my tears until I can ask: "Who did this to you, and why?"

"Ming—with Hu's cigar," he says. "When we first began posting our dances on social media. She was livid when I changed up the choreography. She said this would always remind us that we belonged to them."

Jody puts an arm around each child. "The twins have a big day tomorrow." She looks over at Dominic. "They should come back to Dominic's suite with us," she insists.

"Of course," Dominic murmurs.

Jack waits until they've walked out before calling Arnie and Abu. "Clean-up on Aisle 713."

As we walk back to the elevator, Jack says, "So, if the Lóngs weren't the couriers for Eagle and Snake's exchange with the Murphys, it's got to be Eric and Erica."

"I guess we'll find out tomorrow, along with Mary and Evan." I grab Jack's arm. "I've got a really bad feeling about their mission tomorrow."

Jack stops short. "Hey…isn't that Aunt Phyllis's room?" He points to the right door—

Which, to my dread, seems to be slightly ajar.

I put my finger to my lips to hush him. We draw our guns.

Then we inch closer.

Gently, I nudge the door.

My aunt's stateroom is dark. But the metallic sequins on her dress flicker from the full moon streaming in through her deck door.

Arms and legs akimbo, she lies on her back, her face obliterated by what must have been a shot directly to it.

This doesn't stop me from shouting her name.

Or running to her.

Or clawing Jack away as he tries to stop me from cradling her in my arms as I weep incoherently, all the while blaming myself for not insisting that she go, the tournament be damned.

For not watching over her while she was here.

For taking her for granted.

Silently, Jack stands over me. In time, I realize that no amount of grief or regret will bring her back to me.

Gently, I lay her back onto the floor. "We…can't let the children find her here, like this. We have to tell them," I whisper.

"Yes, of course." Jack helps me to my feet.

Noting that I'm covered in blood, he walks me to the bathroom so that I can wash her blood from my hands. I'm shaking too hard to do the same to my blood-smeared dress. To cover it as best he can, Jack wraps his jacket around me. "Whenever you're ready." The sorrow in his voice pierces my heart, shattering it to pieces.

In time, I take the sluggish steps that will put me in front of those I love most.

I will watch them age with grief because of something that they should not have experienced until fate took Phyllis away, graciously and oh so gently.

Not like this.

Never like this.

My aunt's killers will pay for taking her from us.

13

Photobomb

*P*HOTOBOMBING *IS THE ART OF PRANKING ANOTHER BY positioning oneself behind just as they are in the act of taking a selfie.*

There are a few reasons why you may do something so silly:

First, you and your friends think it's cute to do this to each other. Sure, go for it.

Next, you and your friends think it's a hoot to do this to strangers. Granted said strangers may find it annoying, but hey, you're cute, so why should they mind? Besides, if they give chase, you can run faster, even in heels.

And finally, you're next to one of your celebrity idols, whom you know would never consent to have a photo taken with you (the no-stalking letter with your name on it states plainly why), and as far as you're concerned, the jailtime is worth it.

By the time you get out of the clink, you may feel differently.

Jack has the forethought to call Mary and Evan and ask them to meet us on our floor. He tells them we have an announcement to make.

They are waiting for us by the elevator. When we enter and I push the button to the Presidential deck, instinctively Mary puts her arm around me. She doesn't know why I'm bereft, but she knows me well enough to recognize that my glazed stare and deafening silence signifies the gravity of our announcement.

She also understands that it is more important than the issues that have come between us this past week.

Whatever has happened, we stand united.

Neither Jack nor I speak on the elevator ride to the Prince Charles Presidential deck.

I am relieved to see that Porter is not part of the security detail tasked with guarding the stateroom's exterior door. I would have collapsed from grief. Upon seeing us, the two that are on guard murmur into their mouthpieces. While one opens the door, the other nods us through it.

The soccer team has their sleeping bags spread out all over the floor of the stateroom's formal living room. Coach Kendra walks between them, handing out hydro flasks and protein bars to the girls. When she notices us, her face lights up—

Until she sees that we're too upset to return her smile.

Trisha and Janie sit arm-in-arm in an easy chair, giggling as three girls do an improvised dance routine to some Taylor Swift party song. Janie's Secret Service agents, who stand near a door, can't help but grin at the girls' shenanigans.

But when Trisha sees the look on my face, she untangles herself from Janie and comes over to us. "Mom…is everything okay?"

"There's a bit of family business to discuss. Is there somewhere we can talk in private?" Jack asks.

"Jeff will want to hear this too," I add, looking around for him. "Where is he?"

"In Lee's quarters, watching the Dodgers game." She takes my hand and Jack's and walks us through a small corridor. At the end of it is a closed double door.

Mary and Evan follow us.

WE SEEM TO BE MOVING IN SLOW MOTION.

I know I'm imagining that our footsteps are echoing against the walls. My heartbeat also sounds loud in my ears. Even with all these other sounds amplified, I can still hear the one thought that keeps buzzing around in my head:

Aunt Phyllis is dead… Aunt Phyllis is dead… Aunt Phyllis is dead…

I don't want to tell my children because I know that the moment those words leave my lips, their lives will be branded with a sadness that will never fade.

I glance at Trisha. Despite the solemn set of her lips and the worried gaze in her eyes, I must brace myself for the torrent of grief that will erupt from her when her mind comprehends our horrendous news. I envision her being flooded with memories of all my aunt's kindnesses. I pray that the sound of Phyllis's laugh will never be forgotten; that my children's minds can always summon the vision of her impish smile; that her zest for new experiences will be a driving force for seeking joy and adventure in their own lives.

The realization hits me: my mind is trying to stop time in its tracks.

LIFE IS FILLED WITH TINY TWISTS OF FATE.

Jeff and Lee are cheering on the Dodgers batter who is sweeping the bases. Porter stands behind them, his fists clenched as he too shouts at the umpire who wants to call the tag on the runner as an out.

I don't want to put an end to this moment in time, but I must.

I walk over to the television and turn it off.

The men's dismay goes off like a bomb. Its blast is aimed at me: "What the heck?" and "Why did you do that?" and "Mom, what are you thinking!"

In time, my silence mesmerizes them.

At that point, I summon all the courage I have to speak: "I have some bad news. Mary, Jeff, Trisha, and Evan: Jack and I just came from Aunt Phyllis's cabin." I force myself to scan their faces, to prepare for their pain: "She…she is dead."

No one speaks.

No one moves.

I look at our children: Mary and Evan's faces shift from shock to horror.

Jeff's reflects his confusion.

Trisha's mouth opens as if dragged down by her incomprehension.

And then Aunt Phyllis's head pops out from behind the suite's kitchen door. Gaily, she pronounces: "Okay, who's up for a heart attack on a plate?"

I stare at her, then at Jack.

I know she means the casserole dish of chili cheese fries in her hand.

Still, I faint.

I WAKE WHEN A COLD GLASS OF WATER HITS ME SQUARELY IN the face.

As I snort water, Jack tries to apologize. I shake it off. "Quid pro quo, right?"

At that point, I realize that Aunt Phyllis's arms are cradling me.

I can't stop crying.

Now she's blubbering too.

But soon, we are both laughing instead.

And now Jack and the kids are hugging us and they're laughing too.

And crying.

Porter is shaking his head, stymied.

Lee nudges him. "Told you," he mutters.

I dare to ask: "You told him what?"

Lee snickers. "That someday the Craigs would be the death of us. I guess I just got it the wrong way around."

Jack puts his hand over my mouth before I can tell Lee in which dark, dank hole he can stuff his predictions.

When the chuckles trickle off, Jack turns to Aunt Phyllis. "I'm sorry to tell you but there's a dead body in your cabin —and it's wearing your dress. It even has your bright red hair. The face was blown off, so we assumed it was—"

Phyllis jumps up so hard that she knocks the casserole dish that Porter somehow saved when she dropped onto her knees to comfort me. When it crashes to the floor, chili fries fly all over us. "Oh my God! Joe! It's … poor Joe!"

Trisha sits straight up. "The Poser? But…how—"

"He choreographed a dance for me. It was so much fun that I suggested we dance it together. You know, do it as a double act. That way, we could stream it live on both of our FaceStaTweet accounts. Cross-promote it to our separate audiences and perhaps pick up each other's followers. He loved the idea and was hoping I'd say that. Just in case, he even brought along an identical dress and a wig. I would have hung downstairs with him and done his makeup and hair, but Porter called to tell me that Lee and all the boys had secured the West Coast video feed of the Dodgers game. I wouldn't have missed that for the world!" She looks over at me. "I know I promised you to stay put in my cabin. But then I thought, 'Wouldn't it be safer for me to be here?' So I let Joe have free rein of my makeup stash." With shaking hands, she pulls out her cell phone. She scrolls through her texts until she finds the last one. "See? he sent me a few photos so that I could weigh in on whether he'd gotten my eyebrow pluck just right. I was wondering why he hadn't sent me a final photo with the finishing touches." She wipes away her tears. "Well…now I know."

I move her to a settee. "Phyllis, whoever did this thinks

you're dead. If you want to get off this ship alive, I strongly suggest that you stay that way."

"What?... You mean, drop out of the contest?"

"Trust us, Aunt Phyllis," Jack implores. "These folks mean business."

"But I—"

"No butts, Phyllis," Porter says sternly. "Look, sweetheart: I have to put my life on the line every day. Do you wonder why I change the topic whenever you ask me about my most hair-raising experiences on this job?" He shrugs. "Because reliving them isn't fun. It's like inviting Post Traumatic Stress Syndrome into that part of your brain that reminds you how mortal you really are." He scans the room, at the other agents. "Am I right?"

They stay silent, but their eyes shift away: tacit agreement that the job isn't all guts and glory.

He holds tight to her. "You're the best dancer I know. Hell, you're the best person I know. If I had lost you, I'd..." His voice trails off.

Her hand reaches up to cup his cheek. "Porter Crosby, are you proposing to me?"

He stares down at her. Then he lifts her into his arms and kisses her.

"If I'm going to answer you, it's not going to be here with our families gawking at us," she whispers.

Between here and the kitchen, he only slips once on the chili fries.

Lee declares, "I thought she'd never ask."

Jeff sighs. "It truly is a miracle."

Mary shrugs. "Oh, I don't know. They've felt that way about each other for some time now. I guess the thought of losing the one you love makes you realize how precious it is to have them by your side."

"Exactly," Evan murmurs. He takes Mary's hand. She clenches it like she'll never let it go.

Jeff snorts. "That wasn't the miracle I meant. Anyone could see the writing on the wall with those two. The blessing in disguise was the murder attempt. It gets her off social media." He rolls his eyes. "Some of those trolls can be vicious! Do you know how many times a day I go into her account and block some of those assholes? It was becoming a full-time job."

I pick up Aunt Phyllis's phone where she left it on the floor and click onto the text of the last photo sent by Joe. Beyond his reflection in the mirror, a shadow lurks.

Jack looks over my shoulder. "What are you up to?"

"See that? I think that's an image of the killer. Whoever this is didn't know he'd photo-bombed Joe's selfie."

Jack takes a closer look. "I think you're right. You're going to pass it to Emma?"

"Done," I say with a click. "Now, let's all get some sleep. Eleven in the morning will come soon enough."

And I'll be dreading every second until the exchange is made, and Mary and Evan are in the clear.

14

Listicle

You know those lists that live on practically every website, that begin with a number that tells you how many quick facts you can now learn for those many questions you never thought to ask? In the social media world, those are called "listicles."

Here are a few:

Eight Parenting No-No's.

Twelve Places You'll Want on Your Bucket List.

Twenty-One Ways to Safely Sanitize Your Home.

102 Honest Answers to the Questions Every Husband Wants to Ask, and Every Wife Needs to Know.

My guess: if you saw these listicles somewhere, you'd read each one, just because you're curious to see what you're missing.

And that's the point! You've clicked onto these articles and gotten a few new pointers.

And you've also learned a new word.

∾

179

"Wake up, sleeping beauty." At the sound of my soft, sweet purr, Grady's eyes flutter open.

He's still groggy from that whiff of my sweet-smelling sleeping spray. But seeing me beside his bed in one of the cabin's plush white bathrobes, bent seductively as I straighten the black seam on my—that is, Miss Delish's left gartered stocking—puts a smile on his face—

Until he realizes he's been gagged.

And tied, spread-eagled, to the bed.

And that he's totally exposed—

Not in a *good* way, either.

He then notices what I have in my hand: a stun gun.

Mine, not his little plaything.

I run the stun gun up his leg, ankle to thigh. I stop it just a few inches from his groin.

Then I ask: "Tell me about your relationship with Eagle and Snake."

Grady gives me a tortured look. He's saying something but I can't hear it.

I lean over him to pull the ball gag out of his mouth. "I…I don't know any one named Eagle. Or Snake, for that matter. I once hired a sous chef who went by Vulture. Strange dude—"

"Wrong answer." I pop the gag back into his mouth.

The stun gun's shock is a light one. And yet because it's too close to the family jewels, he yelps like a kitten who got its tail caught underfoot.

"Try again," I suggest.

He frowns. "Is it some restaurant? If it is, and you're looking for a gig, I know people all over the world who'd love to have a high-profile chef. I'll hook you up, I promise—"

Yet again I cram the gag into his mouth. Then, to make the point that now is not the time to conveniently forget his employer, I make a point to show him that I'm upping the amps on my stun gun, so he needs to come clean.

He whines—

Then whimpers when the shock sparks his hair—down there.

"Don't play stupid, Grady."

He's hyperventilating. The choke collar keeps him from shaking his head too much, but he's definitely developed a palsy.

Hmmm…

I pull off the gag so that he can take air in through his mouth. When his breathing slows, I ask, "Where is your cell phone?"

Grady shrugs. "Wherever Justin is. He takes care of my social media—taking photos and videos, posting every-thing—as well as my sponsorship deals, and any niggling little issues that come up with my six restaurants."

Ah! Well, that explains a lot.

"So, he's your go-to guy, eh?"

Grady nods. "Hey, listen, don't get any ideas about stealing him away from me. Since he came onboard, I've made more money than I ever have in my whole life. I'm not just a chef anymore, I'm a brand! I've got sponsorships, I'm opening up restaurants all over the world—"

"Does he get a cut of it?"

"Yeah." Grady snickers. "It was his idea to work strictly on commission. In the beginning, I couldn't pay him, so I was fine with that. What can I say? It's paid off for both of us."

"It may have paid for you to take a one-way ticket to a Federal penitentiary. He's using your social media account to send coded messages to terrorists."

His eyes bulge in shock. "No! … Fuck!... Really? Well, how was I to know?"

"If you didn't, you're in the clear. But I need that cell to clear you."

"Listen, Miss Delish—or whomever you are—I swear I'm telling the truth! I never want to see that lying prick again—"

There's a tap on the door, to *Shave and a Haircut.*

Fear darkens Grady's eyes. "Speaking of the prick—!"

I stick that gag back in his mouth. "Nope, not you. I'll do all the talking. In fact, why don't you relax? You know, take a nap?" Yet again, I spritz him with the sleep spray— but just enough to make him woozy.

His head lolls back and his eyes glaze over, but there's a smile on his lips.

I walk over to the door and look through the peephole.

He's right. Justin is standing there.

I open the door a crack. "Can't you read?" I point to the DO NOT DISTURB sign.

He looks over my shoulder—

To see his boss tied up and humming a slow-motion version of *She's a Dish* by The Hard-Ons.

Oh so appropriate.

Justin takes it all in with a snort. "Well, well, well! Looks like someone had a little too much fun last night. You're a very bad influence on my client, Miss Delish. He's already missed a fan breakfast—*that he was supposed to cook.* And he's due for a lunch with the money men at noon. Think you can untie things up by then?"

"Sure, if you make it worth my while. Like, say, give me a few pointers on raising my Social Media profile?"

He looks down to where my robe finally meets: just below my belly button. "Sure, for a little quid pro quo. In fact, you'd be a great addition to my stable"—he yanks me by the sash of my robe so that we're chest to breast—"of clients."

I lick my lips, as if what he says is catnip to me. "Ooh, sounds interesting. What are you offering, exactly?"

As if I don't already know. By the time his belt is unbuckled, I take the spray from the pocket of my robe—

But instinctively, he slaps it out of my hand.

The vial falls to the floor.

We both scramble for it—

But he grabs it first. "What the hell is this stuff, anyway?" He spritzes it at me.

Seeing how I'm holding my breath, he punches me in the gut.

Gasping for air, I double up. When I can right myself, I see that Justin has backed away. Guffawing, he declares, "Ah, I see! An aerosol roofie, eh? Well, that's certainly convenient." As he glances at Grady, he adds, "Especially if you're not the prettiest bitch in the litter. Frankly, though, I don't know why you thought you'd need it. He's been jonesing for you since the moment he saw you. Go figure, considering all the hotties I'd invited to play with us."

He hasn't noticed that I've taken several steps backward, toward the suite's dining room table.

I've just bumped into it when, suddenly, Justin turns and stares at me. "Ah, I get it!" He wags his finger. "You're not who you say you are. You're Acme."

"Which makes you Eagle and Snake," I retort.

"Which makes you one dead bitch, who—*oops!*—will accidentally fall overboard." In a flash he's at my side. Just as he points the spray at my face, I raise the carving knife that Grady left on the table and, with all my might, I slash Justin's wrist.

They say that practice makes perfect. The skill honed at Grammy Doo's Diner proves valid here too as his severed hand falls to the floor, still clutching the spray bottle.

In the meantime, Justin stares at the blood spurting out of his mangled arm. Angered, he still has the energy to charge at me.

You don't know what you're capable of until you are threatened. His goal is to watch me die alongside him.

Because my goal is to live long enough to meet my children's children, I grab the cleaver and bury it in Justin's forehead.

He crumples onto the floor. The whack, deep in the frontal lobe, paralyzes him.

Not only can he not speak he can't move.

Gone is his ability to feel. To emote. To solve the biggest problem that he currently faces:

How to survive.

He just can't.

To put him out of his misery, I press a pillow to his face.

As his body goes limp, his last gasp has the wistfulness of a disappointed sigh.

I ransack his pockets until I find what I'm looking for: the talking points he was going to give Grady.

I stumble to my feet. After finding my cell, I take a screenshot and forward it to Emma so that ComInt can decipher it.

Then I call Jack.

"You're taking your sweet time," is how he answers.

It's not his fault he hasn't a clue what I've been through. It's not even nine and already I'm exhausted.

I've got to learn how to pace myself.

"By the way, Eric and Erica have moved to another room—under assumed names, apparently."

"Isn't that just peachy keen!" I sigh, then I just come out with it: "I had to exterminate Justin."

"I'm sure Ryan will cry over it, but not me." Jack replies. "Frankly, Don, these guys aren't going to fold. They play for keeps. Well, guess what? We do too."

In other words, it'll be a fight to the finish.

Oh, joy.

15

Disappearing Content

Also known as "ephemeral content," posts that delete themselves after a set amount of time has passed is known as "disappearing content."

Both Snapchat and Instagram offer this feature. It works to the social media platform's favor in that such spontaneity encourages constant participation for fear of missing something really, really, cool. (See Chapter 3 Tip entitled "FOMO.")

But here's the thing, you have already missed out on some great stuff.

Like snorkeling in Fiji.

Or watching the birth of a whale in real time.

Or attending your favorite cousin's college graduation.

There is no way you can be everywhere at once. So, why not just live your life in the moment, and to its fullest?

∼

"You can still back out, you know." I'm helping Mary tuck her naturally brown hair into a wig of long golden blond tresses that, with the mask identical to Candy Murphy's face, complete her disguise as the glamping influencer-turned-treasonous killer. "You've already exposed a terrorist. That proves you've got the right stuff. If you changed your mind now, Mario wouldn't hold it against you."

"I have to do this, Mom. Not just for the success of our mission. I need to prove to myself that I'm up for the task of diplomatic espionage. Otherwise, since Acme hasn't proven that I wasn't the girl in that DeepNude, my future will be reduced to community college and a part-time job at the Hilldale Mall." Mary puts her hands on my shoulders. I flinch, but only because I find it hard to look at the face of the young woman whose fatal fall was preceded by my whack with a scalding skillet of grits.

I force myself to meet her eyes. "I respect your decision. At the same time, please respect my concern. In all my years working for Acme, I've rarely had a mission that went exactly as planned. The courier will be at close range with you. He or she could suspect anything, like the fact that you aren't who you say you are—"

"You don't get it! Evan and I spent the whole night learning everything about the Murphys. No, much more than that. We *are* the Murphys!" As Mary says this, her voice changes into the husky, whiney air-headed cadence that is pure Candy. At the same time, she tosses her hair flirtatiously, as she walks away from me with Candy's sexy saunter—

And that cruel chuckle that made me shudder when Candy was describing how she'd like to kill me.

Grudgingly, I admit, "Okay, yeah, granted, you could be her twin."

"You can thank Jody for that. She worked with us on their better-known mannerisms. She's studied them since they became megas, so that she can pass along the traits that she feels will work for her other clients."

"It's great that you can imitate them so well, Mary. But here's the thing: the Murphys had already been paid for the job. Eagle and Snake isn't going to just let you waltz out of there with another payday."

"Emma and Ryan went over the failsafe with us."

"Oh yeah? What did they say exactly?" You bet I'm as miffed as I sound, and for good reason:

They should have gone over it with Jack and me too.

Mary sighs. "First off, we'll be in the designated cabana two hours early. But even before we get there, Arnie, Abu, Dad, you, and Mario will be electronically scanning everyone around the pool so that ComInt can ID them as civilians who have registered for the event. Anyone who doesn't check out will be tagged for ongoing SecCam surveillance."

I nod grudgingly. "Go on."

"Ten minutes before the allotted time for the hand-off, Dominic and his entourage will not only be in the next cabana but surrounding ours as well. The moment the courier arrives, our computer will be ready to accept the SD card so that the courier can validate the stolen intel. But we won't hand off the computer along with the SD card until he or she transmits the NTF valued at ten million dollars US into a crypto account number that we give them. The minute the nontraceable funds are in the account, Dominic and his uniformed wrecking crew will swarm into our cabana from all sides and Evan and I will slip away with them, disguised in our own Dominic couture, which is under our cabana wear." Rolling her eyes, she lifts her wrap dress, giving me a peek of the gold lamé bikini bottom under it.

"Okay, good," I prompt her. "What then?"

Mary sighs. "We stay put and party like its nineteen-ninety-nine."

"You forgot one thing: to make sure you take off your masks."

Mary chuckles. "Evan and I certainly won't make the same mistake as Dad and try to pull it off the wrong way." She lifts a corner of the mask to prove her point. "Satisfied?"

I shake my head. "Not really. Frankly, I won't be until we're all home, safe and sound." I sigh. "Already the body count on this mission has been too high. And if anything had happened to Aunt Phyllis…"

Mary puts her arm around me. "But it didn't. If anything, it brought her closer to Porter. It made them realize how much they were willing to commit to each other."

"How about you?" I ask. "Have you and Evan been able to work out your differences?"

Mary shrugs. "Not entirely. I mean, yes, he has accepted my decision to follow this through for…well, for as long as it suits me."

As long as you aren't hurt.

Or worse, killed.

In other words, it will never suit me...

"But the thought of my having to...to flirt with other guys...or even... well, you know: have sex with cold-blooded killers..." She looks me in the eye. "How do you and Dad do it, Mom?"

I hold her gaze. "We knew it was part of the job when we took it on. When you were little and your biological father—"

"Carl." Her tone is cold. Blunt.

"Yes, Carl. When he disappeared, I accepted the position because it was my way at getting back at those who took him from me. And the sex...it was just that. Not love. Just...a physical way to get information from an enemy."

Mary nods slowly. "I understand. You've trained your mind to view it as another weapon."

"Exactly."

"I don't know if I could get used to that."

"You don't have to Mary. If you see it as a... a violation. At the time I started this job, I didn't. I had no feelings about... about sex. I guess because I'd lost the love of my life."

"You have a different love now. As does Dad. And yet...neither of you have walked away from that part of the job."

"We've talked about it."

Mary nods. "Well, that's a step in the right direction, I guess."

"Your father is much better at compartmentalizing it— at least, when he's tasked with playing honeypot. But yes, it bothers him when I have to do it."

"Interesting that he doesn't see the double standard he's created."

I snicker. "Yeah, well, trust me. We've had that conversation as well." I shrug. "The mutual understanding is that when one of us calls it quits, we'll quit together."

"Makes sense! I mean, if one of you stayed in the field when the other quits, I would imagine that just knowing what the person you love is submitting to would break you apart..."

Her voice trails off.

She gets it.

She now knows why Evan hates the thought of her joining Jack's and my chosen profession.

"Yes, it's heartbreaking," I murmur. "Now, imagine if you'd lost your loved one this way."

Mary's eyes grow wide. It takes a moment for her to shake off her trepidation. "It's time for me to meet Evan. We'll see you afterward."

She grabs the beach wrap she'll wear over her sun dress and walks out the door without looking back.

MARY AND EVAN ARRIVE AT THEIR CABANA WITH TWO HOURS to spare for their rendezvous with the Eagle and Snake courier. Double rows of these tricked-out tents line the starboard and port sides of the ship.

The meeting is to take place in the last cabana in the left row on the port side. It is one of the bougier cabanas, facing the pool as opposed to looking out over the ocean.

The lounge chairs in front of each cabana are also

attained by reservation only. Dominic's mega-party has done so for all lounge chairs on that side.

A few minutes after Mary leaves, I position myself on a lounge chair directly across the pool from Mary and Evan's cabana, which has one of its flaps pulled to the side. Since I don't want to attract fans, I'm not disguised as Miss Delish. I'm just another sun bunny, wearing oversized sunglasses over my special Acme lenses and a big floppy sun hat over a long auburn wig, which covers the earbuds in which Emma alerts us to the unseen. I chose the shortest sundress in my luggage, just skimming the hemline of my concealed carry shorts. If things kick off, I only need half a second to instantly draw my Sig Sauer P229. Because there are too many civilians around to shoot safely, I've got a hidden pocket for my stun gun too.

Jack, his Dominic mask disguised with a mustache and sunglasses, shows up a moment later. A few minutes afterward, Abu, sans his Sleek Sikh get-up, takes a lounge chair that triangulates Jack's and my position. Arnie is in his cabin, monitoring the ship's security cameras as well as the cameras within the cabana. Within the hour, Dominic and his merry makers have shown up. His arms bow heavily around the women who hang onto him, like a tree bearing too much over-ripe fruit.

As Mary predicted, besides taking over the cabana to the right of where the handoff is to take place, his party has taken over the only cabana immediately next to hers. In fact, as Dominic promised, the revelers have surged all around Mary's cabana, as if they own it too. Since they are all dressed in Dominic's signature attire, it should be easy to pick out the courier.

Soon it's time for the courier to appear. We wait…

And wait…

And wait…

Fifteen minutes after the meeting time, I mutter, "Something is wrong."

"Shall I walk by and casually glance in?" Dominic murmurs back.

"Yes," Jack and I respond together.

He disentangles himself from the scrum of women who have been posing with him and casually backs up until he's in front of the cabana's open flap.

He pauses just a moment before rushing in. A second later, he's shouting "Mayday! Mayday! Man down!"

Evan has been shot in the back. He is slumped down in one of the chairs that face the circular table. His eyes are closed.

The computer is gone, as is the SD card.

And so is Mary.

As Jack, Abu, Mario, and I jump up and run toward the cabana, Arnie screams, "Oh shit! The SecCam in the cabana has been looped since Mary and Evan first went in!"

"How the hell did that happen?" Ryan bellows.

"It wasn't done by me!" Arnie insists.

"Or on our end either!" Emma declares. "Eagle and Snake must have taken the precaution."

The flap between their cabana and the one that flanks it on the ocean side is open. I run through—

But no one is there.

The flap facing the ocean slaps against the tent.

I run out, looking one way, then the other.

"We're receiving your visual," Emma responds. "Mary's been blindfolded! Otherwise we'd be able to see through her lenses where they're taking her. Right now, my team is scanning all of the deck's SecCam video for the past twenty minutes, to see if we can find Mary's abductors."

In the meantime, Jack is checking Evan for a pulse. He must have found one because he's slapping our ward's face and cajoling him to come to.

At the same time, Abu examines the robe's bullet hole. Puzzled, he raises it from the back.

As directed, Evan wears his Dominic signature tux jacket beneath it.

It too has a bullet hole.

Abu takes a closer look at the entry hole. Suddenly, he pulls out a Swiss Army knife and cuts open one of the arm seams. His eyes widen: "Hey, this tux has a built-in Level Three Kevlar threat vest!"

"But of course it does!" Dominic huffs. "It's a wardrobe must-have for the well-dressed international man of mystery. Slimming as well. Not that I need to worry about that myself—"

"Pain… in…neck…" Evan groans.

"Agreed," I mutter. "Still, he just saved your life, so…" Bending down beside him, I stroke his head and whisper, "Thank God—yes, you are alive!" Just saying that fills me with relief—

Until I remember that Mary is gone.

"Evan, whoever met with you took Mary with them," Mario exclaims.

Evan bolts up. Looking around he declares, "They'll kill her—at least the guy will!"

"*They*? Was it a man *and* a woman?" Jack asks.

Evan nods.

"Eric and Erica," I declare.

"No," Evan insists. "At least…I don't think so because they were wearing disguises. But they weren't built like the dancers. The couriers were heavier. Older too." He holds his head in his hands. "When the bullet hit my back, the force sent me headfirst into the table. Jeez, what a headache!"

"We can't waste time," Jack insists. "Emma, what are you seeing?"

Emma exclaims, "Donna, Mary is with Jody, safe and sound in her cabin.

I am so relieved that I collapse against the wall. In an instant, Evan is at my side. He too has tears of joy in his eyes. "But how? …"

"They'll explain when you get there," she assures me.

"I'm on my way!" I kiss Evan, then Jack—

Then Dominic. He blushes. "Well…now *that* was unexpected."

"If you're surprised by that, then this should knock the wind out of you. I'll take two of those jackets for both my guys. Dominic, finally, your vanity has paid off for the rest of us."

"Would you also like me to put in an order for one of my new Kevlar evening gowns? For obvious reasons, it fits like a glove…" He looks me over. "Then again, perhaps not—Kevlar has yet to address the issue of the lumps and bumps suffered by the more mature woman—"

He stops when he sees me glowering at him.

However, I resist the urge to box his ears.

I'd much rather hug my daughter.

I'VE BARELY TAPPED ON THE DOOR OF JODY'S CABIN WHEN IT swings open. Mary flings herself into my arms.

"Oh, Mom!" Her sobs make her next words almost incomprehensible. "Evan... They—"

"I know, darling, I know. They shot him." I stroke her hair. "He's alright, Mary—except for a headache from hitting his head on the table. It turns out that Dominic's tuxes are bulletproof."

Mary's jaw drops. "Wow! But thank God!" She shakes her head in awe. "These lame bikinis are anything but. They barely cover what they're supposed to, let much less deflect a bullet."

"With Dominic, I have a feeling that's the whole point." I look over at Jody. "How did you get her away from her captors?"

"I just happened to be at the right place at the right time. I knew that Dominic and his fans would be partying poolside, so I decided to stay in my cabin until the reverie was over. When the elevator reached our floor, 'Candy Murphy' was standing there, but her head was down so far that I couldn't see her face. A woman was standing behind her—but uncomfortably close. I only recognized Mary because of her hat. It's one we bought together at the gift shop. I knew something had gone wrong. I didn't know if the woman had a gun on Mary or what. But I got onboard, then pushed the button to the lowest floor. But before the elevator door closed, I yanked Mary out of it with me. At the same time, I sprayed the woman's sunglasses with my tanning spray. She was sputtering and couldn't see a thing."

"Then we ran all the way back to Jody's and locked the door." Mary smiles up at Jody. "You saved my life!"

Jody pats her arm. "I'm sure you would have done the same for me."

Mary frowns. "I'd like to think so. But when you've got a gun pointed at the small of your back, all you can think about is… well, is why you're in that predicament in the first place."

"Thank goodness she wasn't stupid enough to shoot that gun in the elevator. It might have ricocheted and hit her instead," I point out.

"Frankly, I think she was over her head in this whole business. I could tell she didn't want to be there with the man who shot Evan."

"So, she wasn't the one who shot him?" I ask.

Mary shakes her head. "The guy had a heavy accent. Russian, I think. Certainly some Slavic dialect."

"What else can you tell me about him?" I ask.

He's about Dad's age: tall, broad-shouldered, and physically fit. He held himself very formally, but with ease."

"Possibly former military," I surmise.

"He wore a hat and sunglasses, so I couldn't see the color of his eyes," Mary continues. "He had a square jaw. His hair was cropped very close to his head. But it had to be blonde, or white. So were his teeth, which were so even that I'm sure they were capped." Mary holds up her cell. "When he walked in, I hit the transmission app so that Acme could read his texts."

"Was that helpful, Emma?" I ask.

"I'll say! He was the mystery transmission on the plane. You remember, the one that was standing next to Jack and Hansley."

"So, the Eagle and Snake investor was there after all!" I exclaim.

"Hansley may have been about to divulge his name to Jack right before she was killed," Emma reminds me. "As expected, his texts are coded. ComInt is trying to break the cipher now. In the meantime, Jack, Abu, Arnie, Mario and Dominic have posted themselves on various decks. They'll sniff him out."

"Sniff?" Mary shudders. "That's for sure. Talk about the right word for his lady friend."

"Why do you say that?" I ask.

"Her perfume was horrendous! Seriously pee-yew!" Mary holds her nose. "When she left with me, she shoved my hat down over my eyes. The way she stunk, I just wish she'd covered my nose too."

"Stunk?" *Hmmm.* "Did it smell like…Oh, I don't know, maybe sewage?"

Mary nods.

"Penelope!" I growl.

Mary frowns. "You mean Mrs. Bing?"

"Do I ever!"

Her eyes grow wide. "Ha! No wonder she kept poking me with her gun and telling me she couldn't wait to use me as target practice!"

"Come again?" I know Penelope hates me, but she could have never known it was Mary impersonating Candy Murphy.

"Cheever has a crush on Candy," Mary divulges.

Slack jawed, I exclaim, "Wow... *Really?*"

Mary crosses her heart. "Scout's honor. Jeff will be the first to tell you...well, not *you*, Mom, but Evan. And of course, Evan told *me* that Cheever boasts that ... well, euphemistically speaking, Candy burps his worm like nobody else!"

"In his dreams," I mutter.

"Exactly," she exclaims.

I kiss Mary's forehead. "Stay put here until Emma gives you the all-clear. In the meantime, I'm going to have some one-on-one time with our nasty-smelling neighbor."

For a very good reason:

Penelope Bing held my daughter at gunpoint.

Penelope Bing let my ward get a bullet in the back.

Penelope Bing is aiding and abetting terrorists.

For some reason, none of this surprises me.

But, boy, do I have a surprise in store for Penelope Bing.

First things first. I've got to be someone who Penelope will let into her inner sanctum:

Miss Delish.

16

Direct Message

A PRIVATE MESSAGE SENT OR RECEIVED VIA ANY OF YOUR SOCIAL *media accounts to another account on the same platform is known as a "direct message," or by the initials "DM."*

Usually, they are short and sweet.

Mostly, they are from folks you know, and have "friended" on the platform.

Occasionally, they are not so sweet. In fact, some are down-right vulgar.

Usually, these come from someone you don't know.

Trust me: you don't want to know them, either.

If you receive one and you don't recognize the sender, it's because they are "phishing." In other words, they hope you'll respond. Doing so may allow them to hack and hijack your account.

Bottom line: don't engage others you don't know unless you like to walk on the wild side.

Or if you don't mind losing access to your online life.

"WE'VE TRACKED PENELOPE TO CABIN NUMBER 522," EMMA says. "It's the one registered to her."

She's read my mind: I'm on the warpath.

"Cheever's cabin is on another floor," she continues.

"Of course it is. Mommy Dearest wouldn't want him interfering with her trysts with their new sponsor—Eagle and Snake. How is the facial recognition going for the Russian investor?"

"Slow," Emma admits. "Like Penelope and Mary, after he shot Evan, he escaped through the ocean view cabana. But he headed straight into the crowd, where I'm sure he ditched his disguise because we never picked him up again."

"Can you pull up footage from the private plane, or from the tarmac when we landed at BWI?"

"We're searching it now. Whereas we've come across a man with similar proportions and gait a few times, he's an expert at hiding his face."

I think for a moment. "Hey—Jack must have seen Mystery Man! Perhaps when Hansley was standing between them on the plane?"

"That's just it. Jack was adjacent to Mystery Man, but Jack swears Hansley wasn't with anyone else. All we can figure is that there must have been one of the plane's flimsy partitions between them."

"Ah, got it. I'll bet that Mystery Man could hear Hansley's conversations with the other investors and sponsors, which was helpful to him regarding negotiations with the influencers that he's got his eye on."

At least we know one person who has seen him—

And knows him intimately:

Penelope.

And I know just how to make her talk.

When I get in the elevator, I push the button that takes me to the lowest deck.

"You've gone too far," Emma warns me.

"Nope. In fact, I haven't gone far enough."

ALL FOOD SERVICE COMES FROM THIS AREA OF THE SHIP.

No one stops the celebrated Miss Delish from sashaying her way through the kitchen to talk to the chefs, take selfies with them, then ooh and ahh over their divine cuisine on a video reel or two and also ask for a few cooking tips while live streaming to an audience that is hungry for soundbites on great grub.

The kitchen staff thinks nothing of me pushing a cart to the elevator with me.

Two servings of Lobster Thermador lie beneath the main course's silver dome. Another dome covers a Baked Alaska. A Caesar Salad is also on the cart, along with a silver bucket, icing a bottle of Champagne. I slip a few items that may come in handy under the cart's skirt: a couple of carving knives, a vinegar atomizer, a pot of steaming hot coffee—

Ah, just the ticket! A butane chef's torch.

If Penelope is stupid enough to stand by her man, for once I have no problem in letting her go up in flames.

~

Miss Delish knocks on Penelope's door.

A shadow covers the peephole. She's looking out. I wave gaily at her, then declare: "I thought we two glamorous gals might chat over a scrumptious lunch! In fact, I've invited Cheever to join us." I lift the lid on the lobster.

"Oh?... really?" Penelope is flattered—

Enough so that even her faux pas with Mystery Man has gone right out of her flighty little brain. She opens the door, sporting her Blue Steel smile. "Well then, yes, come on in."

I push the cart into the cabin. Then, silently I close the door behind me.

~

She still holds a damp cloth to her face. Her eye is swollen from the suntan oil that Jody sprayed at it.

"Tsk, tsk," I murmur. "Bee sting, perhaps?"

"Um...no. It was that slut, Candy Murphy! You know her, right? She's a glamping influencer. We had a bit of a tiff—over my son, Cheever—and the bitch had the nerve to squirt her cheap suntan oil in my face!"

"Nerve is right!" I murmur. "Maybe you girls should oil up and catfight it out! Imagine the eyeballs for that event! You'd break FaceStaTweet!"

"No!... I... I'm too much of a lady for that."

Give me a break. She's only passing because she knows she'd lose.

"I have to stay dignified, for Cheever's sake." She

raises her head proudly. "Unfortunately, my little guy has got a bit of a crush on her. Frankly, she's much too old for him. She's nearly my age!"

Liar. The girl was twenty-four, tops.

Of course, in Penelope's mind, she's still twenty-four too. Talk about a case of arrested development.

"I know just the trick for that," I say. "Go ahead and have a seat." I motion to the chair by the deck door. "Now, let's get that eye back to normal. No need to have the platform lighting up with the hashtag 'Cyclops,' right?"

Like an obedient little girl, she does as I ask.

I pull the chef's torch and a knife from the cart's shelf, then heat the knife with the torch until I know it's hot enough—

To brand Penelope if she does anything stupid.

Like trying to withhold the information I need about her very bad boyfriend.

"This may hurt, just a little," I purr.

Then place the scorched knife against her bare shoulder.

When she screams, I sock her in the face.

She falls to the floor. At least that shuts her up.

As she lays there whimpering, I straddle her. I grab a handful of her hair. Holding the torch's flame next to it, I growl, "Okay, listen up Penelope, and listen good. That man who you think is your next big meal ticket is really a Russian terrorist with a mission to disable our government tonight. If you don't tell me where he is right this very second, you'll either end up in the cell next to him in Gitmo, or worse yet face a firing squad for treason."

The U.S. no longer uses firing squads. I don't even know if women are housed in Gitmo.

I do know that if anything happens to my family on this ship, she's sleeping with the fishes.

I'll make sure of that.

"Miss Delish, I can't tell you! He'll kill me!"

"What, and you don't think I won't? I'm not a doctor. I don't even play one on TV. Trust me, this is the worst kind of plastic surgery for someone who spends as much money as you do for nips and tucks." I touch the flame to the knife again. This time I put it so close to her cheek that she digs her face deep into the floor's plush carpeting.

She's shivering.

She is scared.

Good. I want her to be shaking in her boots.

"Okay—okay! I'll tell you what I know, but it isn't much." Her lip trembles.

"Oleg Petrov approached me with a fantastic sponsorship deal for my son, Cheever Bing. Not only will he win the tournament but fifty million dollars immediately goes into Cheever's crypto account."

"And what does Baby Bing have to do to earn this payoff?"

Penelope scoffs. "What he always does: read, verbatim, something that Oleg wants him to say to his followers. Easy-peasy."

"When will Cheever be getting this missive?"

"Not until right before he's to go into the tournament." She shrugs. "And the way the other contestants are dropping out—make that *dropping dead*—he may win by default. You know, the last influencer standing. So, not only will he win the prize money, but he'll also have Oleg's bonus to boot."

"It doesn't make for much of a tournament," I mutter.

"Oleg doesn't really care about that. And quite frankly, neither do I—especially when I deliver you to him. He's angry that I let Candy Murphy get away."

Suddenly, she slaps the torch out of my hand. Then, with all her might, she raises up —

Shoving me over.

I fall to one side, knocking the cart over—

And giving her time enough to get on her feet. From her jacket pocket, she pulls out the gun she used on Mary.

My glasses have been knocked off my face. She pulls off my wig and cap, then gasps at who she sees before her:

The one person who she hates more than anyone else.

Well, the feeling is mutual.

Triumphantly, she crows, "I thought I recognized your voice, Donna Craig! Once again, you're trying to ruin my chance to give Cheever the life he deserves. Only this time, I won't let you. I'll shoot to kill. Believe me, I'll enjoy ridding Hilldale—for that matter, the world—of you, so don't get any bright ideas."

"Sorry, Penelope, but I think you're helping him end up right where he truly belongs—*in jail.*"

She's so angry at my jibe that she takes aim with the gun—

But at the same moment, I grab the dome lid and point it in her direction.

The bullet goes in, only to ricochet back out. Frightened she turns away—

Just as it zips past her, shattering the glass door behind her—

And showering Penelope with its shards.

She screams when she sees blood from the cuts all over her body.

"My face! … I must be dying!" She moans.

"You're overreacting. They're surface wounds—"

"Shut up, you! Once again, you've ruined me!"

"You did it to yourself, Penelope. And sadly, because of your greed, you're taking Cheever down with you."

My punch is hard enough to knock her into the wall.

When she drops, it's face first onto the floor.

There's a knock on the door. If it's Oleg or one of his goons, I'll have to think quickly—

"Need more room service in there?"

Yet again, I'm so happy to hear my dear husband's sweet, deep baritone.

I swing open the door.

Jack's got Arnie with him. He's toting a laundry cart. "Do you think she'll fit in here?" Jack asks.

I shrug. "She's limp enough now. And considering all the yoga and Pilates she does, I assume she's flexible too. Do your best to shove her in there while we search the cabin for anything that may be of help in figuring out the fireworks planned for tonight."

"Emma has secured an empty cabin under an assumed name. It has a permanent DO NOT DISTURB message to the Prince Charles's reception desk. We can tie her up, spritz her with the sleeping spray, and let her sleep it off in there," Jack explains. "We'd planned on using it as a brig for the terrorists, but we seem more adept at killing our suspects than detaining them."

Arnie is rummaging in Penelope's handbag. "Hey, she's got a room card to one of the VIP suites. I wonder whose it is…"

It hits us at the same time, but Jack utters it first: "Mystery Man's."

Arnie grabs Penelope's cell phone from her bag and shifts her against the wall. Then, with one hand on the phone, he takes the thumb and middle finger of his other hand and lifts her eyelids so that they can be scanned by the device. When the phone goes live, he hoots with joy. "We're in, folks! But I've got to say: I miss the good ol' days when I had to guess some mother's pass code! If it wasn't their kid's name, it was his birthdate."

Note to self: time to change my cell's pass code.

(*Hmmm:* would it be too obvious to go with my porn name? Not any I've used in the past, but the one from that game: you know, your first pet's name and the street you grew up on? Could Arnie do a deep dive on that criteria? Not without Emma's help. And she's no traitor, so all is safe…)

Arnie is swiping through Penelope's pictures—until one stops him cold. "Well, well, well! Look what we have here!" Triumphantly, he hands over the cell so we can see too:

A sex video—of Penelope:

With Oleg. At least, from the description we've been going by.

It's also the side profile of the killer in Joe the Poser's mirror, who shot the poor guy at close range.

"Want to take a guess if he knows she took it?" Jack asks.

"My answer: no," I reply. "Knowing Penelope, she was going to blackmail him with it."

"I wonder how well that would have gone over?" Arnie muses.

"Not at all," Jack and I retort.

I enlarge the photo:

Yep, there it is: the Eagle and Snake tattoo, next to his groin.

Jack lets loose with a low whistle. "We're about to catch one of the biggest fish in the *Orel i Zmeya* pond."

I snicker. "Well then, we better have some really tasty bait."

Jack's smile fades. "Honey, that would be you."

17

Tag (You're it!)

To "tag" someone is to include their account name on your social media posts—either texts or photos—so that those who follow them see your post as well. It's a great way for new followers to find you!

Of course, the last thing you'd want to do is to tag someone who is doing something that will reflect badly on you. For example:

If they're being silly, no need to shine a spotlight on something that would make you look dumb too. Or as Forrest Gump's mama so eloquently put it, "Stupid is as stupid does."

If they are doing something illegal, no need to tag them, let alone bring the photo to light—unless you want to be tried as an accomplice.

If they are doing something despicable, I'd suggest that you not only forgo posting the act but that you drop the friendship too.

It is true that we are judged by the company we keep—no

matter how many followers their social media accounts may have.

WHILE ARNIE WHEELS THE ZIP-TIED AND SLEEP-SPRITZED Penelope down to the brig, Jack and I take the elevator to my suite. When we open the elevator door, Dominic, Evan, Mary, and Jody are already in there. Immediately, they surround Dominic's doppelganger—a.k.a., Jack—to give him cover. And in case anyone is watching, the social media stars among us laugh, talk, and post selfies as we enter Miss Delish's room—

But the moment we're inside, the cameras go off and we go into Jack's more spacious suite to call Ryan.

Mario is already waiting for us. No surprise there. He's already on the phone with Ryan.

"You've got only two hours before the tournament officially begins," our boss warns us. "And whereas Acme's brilliant ComInt team has deciphered Oleg's code, there was nothing in his texts and emails that indicates Eagle and Snake's mission, or the missive that will be relayed by Cheever."

"However, there is one message about the Murphys," Emma adds. "Oleg has texted China's Ministry of Security Services that he now has the SD card, and will hand it over the moment he gets off the ship."

"Who is the contact?" I ask.

"All we've got is the name 'Mr. Rex,'" Ryan replies. "We'll have eyes and ears on Oleg from the moment he leaves the tournament until he gets into his limo to be driven away. And that's where you come in, Donna."

Yikes.

"Oleg has been texting Penelope, ordering her to bring Candy to his suite," he continues.

Double yikes.

Mary looks down at her feet.

"No way in hell," I mutter.

"I agree wholeheartedly that we don't allow 'Candy,'—and by that, I mean Mary—anywhere near him," Ryan declares. "However, if you were to go instead, as Candy—and make a deal with him—"

"What kind of deal? He already has what he wants: the SD Card," I point out. "He took it from Evan-slash-Randy when they were in the cabana."

"Tell him that you got away from Penelope by disarming and murdering her. And that you eliminated Justin too because the Murphys were upset that he was getting all the choice assignments. Remind Oleg that he's got only you to count on."

"And the elusive Eric and Erica," Jack reminds him.

"By having Donna infiltrate Oleg's inner circle, we can track and trace them too—and bring them down before they pull off the tournament's big finale. You'll need to convince him that, with your help in keeping Cheever infatuated with you, Oleg can keep using him as an unwitting operative. And, as an added incentive you'll also tell him that you know where Acme's Jack Craig is holed up; that you're willing to turn him over—for a price."

"And what would that be?"

"You stay an Eagle and Snake asset."

Shite.

Nope. Ain't happening.

"First, you're nuts if you think I'll put Jack in the crosshairs of a known assassin," I exclaim. "And you're doubly wacked if you think I'm going to stay 'Candy' for the rest of my life! No way!" Agitated, I circle the room. If Ryan is looking through my lenses, I hope I'm making him dizzy.

"It won't be the rest of your life. It won't even be after tomorrow. It'll only be until he turns the SD card over to the MSS. After that, he's expendable."

"But by then, Jack will have been 'expended'—by me, no less! And maybe I will have been expended too, for that matter."

Ryan is silent for far too long. And then: "Why now, Donna?"

I frown. "I don't understand your question."

"I'm asking why you're afraid to do your job now?"

Everyone stares at me.

But the only one's eyes I can't meet are Mary's.

"Because…"

I can't say it. Not out loud.

First Carl. Now Jack. I can't do that to my daughter: leave her fatherless yet again.

And, perhaps motherless too.

Which might just happen if something goes wrong.

Not after she just saw the one person who she hopes to spend the rest of her life with—Evan—almost get killed.

Ryan sighs. "I'm waiting."

I can't talk. I can barely breathe.

Mary puts her hand on my arm. "You can do it," she whispers.

She can't know what I'm thinking. If she did, she'd understand why I'm so very afraid.

She leans into me and murmurs, "We'll take care of you."

But no:

I take care of her.

Everyone I love is right here, right now, on this ship with me. If I let Oleg get away with his scheme, we are all doomed.

And our country will somehow be crippled.

This very moment, the best way I can take care of us is to take out Oleg.

"I'm not afraid," I tell Ryan. "Let's do this."

I am the last person Oleg expects to see.

That is to say, *Candy* is a total surprise when I—*she*—saunters toward his front door.

He answers his own door. As I'd suspected, he doesn't hide behind a barrage of tough guys. Nor does he have an entourage kowtowing to him.

The smirk on his face belies the suspicion in his eyes.

And yet he lets me walk through the door.

I guess he thinks he can take me, what with his height, build, strength, and weaponry.

As he frisks me—somewhat intimately—he sees I'm equipped with no more than the body of an angel, the face of a woman he wants to kill, and some misplaced moxie.

I know what he's thinking: *No contest.*

Here's hoping that my opening line evens the odds a bit—in *my* favor:

"Your whore, Penelope, is dead. I threw her overboard. She was as useless as my idiot husband. Now that we're rid of the dead weight, let's tie up the loose ends."

He snorts as if I've said the funniest thing he's ever heard. "You *are* the loose end, my dear Candy." He lets his tongue draw out the "y" in her name.

Good. He's intrigued.

"I'm your best hope for pulling this caper off, and you know it." I toss Candy's luscious white-blond hair and flash her dimples. "The Lóngs are long gone. That simpleton, Penelope, is fish food—which means that pissant son of hers will be the loosest cannon on this tug"—I pucker into a pout—"unless I give him his marching orders. I'm sure that hag of his mother told you about his crush on me."

"Ha! Is that why she hated your guts?" He chortles. "Makes sense now." He looks me over appraisingly. "You will break his cherry."

I lean into him. "Your wish is my command. I'll even let you watch me do it."

Suddenly, Oleg's mouth is on mine, like a vacuum cleaner.

So are his hands, working me over like an octopus having a field day with a school of minnows.

I shove him away. "Then again, maybe you don't deserve any Candy."

He scowls. "Oh, yeah? Why not?"

"Come on, let's face it. Anyone who let Jack Craig slip

out of"—I take his hand and stroke his palm—"these long, strong fingers can't be all that tough."

To make my point I suck his middle finger.

That does the trick.

His eyes go all drowsy, like a dog getting its belly scratched.

Oleg shoves me onto the bed, then falls on top of me—

But not quick enough. I roll out from under him.

"So now you've got an Acme agent roaming the ship," I point out. "Did you know he's already exterminated Justin?"

Seething, he yanks me back toward him. "How do you know this?"

"Justin's client, Grady McDougall, was bemoaning the human sausage he found in his kitchen this morning. It's why Chef Boy-ar-Dee has been out to lunch all day. He's too upset to make the tournament." I put on a sad face and wipe my eyes of fake tears. "Of course, I could convince him otherwise. I have him eating out of my hand. Just pass me McDougall's talking points."

Oleg slams his fist on the wall. "I'd already given it to Justin. The transmissions are always wiped clean afterward." He seethes at the thought of this lost opportunity.

"ComInt has it," Arnie whispers into my earbud. "Decoding it now."

In sympathy with Oleg, I cluck my tongue. "On the other hand, considering you're now left with just Cheever and your flatfooted dance duo, Eric and Erica, I'd say you need me just as much—if not more—than I need you."

His eyes narrow. "What do you want?"

"To win the tournament, of course. And your heart and

soul." To make my point, I clutch the one thing that's neither, but just as hard. "Oh, and another ten million."

Oleg shakes his head. "It's already been decided. Cheever will win."

"I'll bet Eric and Erica don't know that."

Suddenly his hands are around my neck. "And they won't either, if you know what's good for you. Everyone has a part to play in this delicate farce on humankind."

Despite the lack of oxygen, I smile. "Oh, baby, you bet I know what's good for me," I purr.

I tighten my grip.

He loosens his. From his inside jacket pocket, he pulls out a folded sheet of paper and hands it to me.

I keep quiet because I already know what he's going to say:

"You run the boy from now on." He licks my neck. "And I run you."

I slap him. The sound reverberates through the room. His face is now marked with the shape of my hand.

I shove him off. "Not until Craig is dead. Remember?"

"You'll pay for that," he snarls.

"Of course I will. And we'll both enjoy every minute of it," I coo. Then coldly, I add: "I've taken over Penelope's suite. I'll lure Craig there."

Oleg nods. "I want to watch."

"A voyeur, a glutton for punishment, and a sadist? My dear Oleg, you are my dream man!" Gently I touch the mark I left on him. "The door will be unlocked. Wait for my text."

This time, when I get off the bed, he doesn't stop me.

18

Metaverse

MANY PEOPLE WOULD ENJOY A FULL RETREAT INTO A VIRTUAL *world. You know, leave the drudgery of the all too real physical world behind.*

They want what has been coined, the "metaverse."

In the Universe—that is, the real world—we do our best to be clear-eyed.

Those who prefer the metaverse look through this millennium's version of rose-colored glasses—Occulus headsets—to block out reality for their CGI version of it.

In the Universe, we come in all shapes, sizes, and colors.

In the metaverse, we are Barbies and Hunks in all forms of cosplay and hairstyles.

In the Universe, we win some and lose some.

In the metaverse, we always win.

Those who prefer the Metaverse believe it is the closest thing to heaven on Earth.

At least, their version of Earth.

The rest of us realize that creating a wonderful universe is a task that will take several lifetimes.

So, are you in?

"I DON'T THINK YOU GOT WHAT HE MEANT," JACK IS telling me.

"Oleg's English is perfect," I insist. "Okay, perhaps a shadow of an accent—"

"Mrs. Craig, you're not listening to me." Nothing drives me up a wall (in a *bad* way) quicker than Jack's know-it-all tone—

Which usually leads to a fight—

Which invariably leads to makeup sex—

Which has me climbing the wall again—

But in a *good* way…

"Donna, wipe that smirk off your face. I'm being serious," Jack insists. "Oleg wants us to put on a show! Then he wants the honor of killing me—possibly during the show. If you remember, my untimely demise was supposed to be on your honey-do list, not his."

"Pshaw! He told me himself that he's a voyeur. Hey, here's a laugh: he wants to watch me do it with Cheever."

"You better hope Cheever doesn't find out. He'd sell tickets for it."

"If he does, I'll wash his mouth out with soap."

Jack shrugs. "He'd probably enjoy that too."

I roll my eyes. "Okay, back to reality. Let's just say you're right. How do we handle it?"

"Well, since neither of us has ever worked in porn I

suggest we don't start now. In fact, I can unequivocally say that having a guy sitting in a corner with a gun aimed at my back may cause my very first case of erectile disfunction."

"We can't let your perfect record be broken." Yes, I'm being sarcastic. "I'd probably have to fake it too—albeit it wouldn't be the first time."

"Your ill-timed honesty is refreshing," he mutters.

I tweak Jack's nose. "Not with *you*, honey!"

Relief breaks out on Jack's face.

Briskly, I declare: "Well, now that the worst version of Truth or Dare is over, here's how I suggest we handle it: when he walks in on us, we should already be in the throes of passion—but dressed—at least, partially—and on the deck. Then I'll shoot you with a gun that has blanks. At the same time, you'll break a fake blood capsule or two, so that he thinks I've effectively accomplished the task. I'll then shove you off the deck into the water. That way, he doesn't get a chance to examine your body."

"And at the same time, I'll hold my breath underwater while he waits for my body to bob up."

"See? Already, the idea is growing on you!" I kiss him. "Now let's practice the 'throes of passion' part. But we'll have to hurry. We don't have much time."

Jack shakes his head. "That part we have down pat. I'm more concerned about the choreography of my untimely demise."

"How Shakespearean," I sniff. "But hey, okay, if it makes you feel better…"

~

"Your lily-white Russian is on his way," Emma murmurs.

That's Emma's warning that Oleg is in the elevator and that we should expect him to come through the door any moment now.

Oh, goody.

Jack has dressed for the swan dive in black tie and expensive shoes, despite the plan that they'll end up waterlogged.

And thank goodness, the Dominic mask is gone. Otherwise, I don't think I could keep a straight face, and that would blow our mission to smithereens.

For both of us.

Emma's warning gets us into position. Jack and I have spent the past hour trying out various up-close-and-personal combinations. We've finally settled on the one I insist will look the most realistic:

We will be making love standing up. Jack's back will be against the deck rail, which means my back will be to the door and Oleg. The minute Jack sees Oleg looking at us, he'll whisper "Now!" in my ear.

When I shoot the gun, the sound effect will be realistic to that of a suppressor. At the same time, beside the supposed bullet's entry point Jack will pierce a packet containing dark red fluid that looks convincingly like blood. When Jack gives a death rattle, I'll push him overboard. As a former member of the US Air Force's Special Tactics force, he's a great swimmer as well as a combat pilot.

"The door is opening," Jack murmurs in my ear.

We go into a deep kiss, but Jack's head is tilted so that he can see over mine, and his eyes are only half-closed.

He's got long lashes so he can pull off that look of desire that women hope for when they open their eyes to take a good look at the great kisser who has them in his arms.

"He sees us," Jack whispers.

I ready the gun I've got against Jack's abdomen—

But then the next thing I know Jack has grabbed me and moved me so that I, not he, is now up against the rail.

When Oleg's bullet hits Jack's back, he gasps and clutches me tight—

Horrified, I push him away.

He lands chest-down against the rail. Blood darkens his jacket, but it doesn't obscure the hole from the bullet that has taken the light from his eyes.

That cut off his last breath.

That has taken the life of the man I love.

I reach for Jack, but it's too late:

He topples overboard.

I stare at his body. It rocks face down in the gentle waves created by the anchored ship.

Our love—

Cannot end like this.

I can't walk out of here. I can't gather my children to my side and tell them how I watched their father get shot—

And that there was nothing I could do to save him.

No. The truth is that I did nothing *to* save him.

But I can still avenge his death.

I feel Oleg's presence beside me. "We fuck now," he growls.

With a quick tap, I've switched off my Acme earbuds and lenses.

Now, no one can see what I do next:

With one quick turn, I jerk my knee into his groin.

As he drops onto the deck, I hiss, "No. You go fuck yourself. Jack Craig was mine, remember?" From my pocket I pull the missive I'm supposed to give to Cheever. Holding it high, I let it flutter in the breeze.

He can't talk, but he wheezes: "*Don't*! Cheever must… I promise I will not…*interfere!*"

So that he keeps his vow, I reach down, and grab hold of his nuts. Twisting them with all my might, I vow, "You better believe you won't."

I put the gun up against them.

He lays there, whimpering in pain. But his eyes dare not meet mine.

I could do it now: kill him.

Afterward, I could shove his body overboard, and there would be no way that Acme would know why or how he disappeared.

Of course, Ryan would easily guess that Jack was the *why*.

And that I was the *how*.

He'd retire me from the field, but Acme would always be watching; waiting for me to go rogue.

To somehow, avenge Jack's death.

So, instead, I move the gun away.

In time, Oleg stumbles to his feet. He groans as he walks gingerly to the front door.

I don't turn to watch him go. Instead, I look out onto the water. Jack's body has slipped under its shiny dark surface.

I feel Oleg's eyes on me. I know he is itching to put a bullet in my back, just as he did to Jack.

But he knows better. I'm the key to his mission's success.

At least, that's what he thinks.

And now I must decide when, and how, to tell my children about Jack's death.

I think I'll wait until after the mission is over—

If they, and I, make it out alive.

Marcus may not get his wish that Oleg lives to tell tales about Eagle and Snake.

I CANNOT STAY IN PENELOPE'S CABIN.

I wait ten minutes, then I run to the elevator, taking it back up to my room.

To be alone.

Not there, but in Jack's suite.

It was there that we last made love.

It was there that I can still smell him; that I feel his presence.

I stand in the living room, envisioning us as we snuggled on the couch.

I see him looking out onto his large deck.

I hear his laugh.

But no, my mind is playing tricks on me. *I will never hear it again.*

Or feel his prickly five o'clock shadow against the back of my hand.

I walk into the bedroom. A shirt lies on the floor. Jeans hang over the back of a chair.

My eyes blur from my tears. Then I remember that I must wipe them away so that the face I must inhabit for the rest of this mission—Candy's face—isn't marred by my negligence.

The same carelessness that took Jack away from me.

The thought makes me wail louder.

At the realization that I will never feel him inside me again, I fall onto the bed, curling up and tucking my legs high to my chest.

Even when your loved one isn't there, do you always feel him by your side?

I feel Jack.

I hear him, now.

Humming off-key. ...

Gently, as if he is so far away.

No—

It's as if he's in the next room.

The bathroom, to be precise.

The water is running.

No... It has stopped.

Emotions surge through me: surprise, fear—

Hope.

Slowly I turn around and see him:

One hand holds the towel wrapped around his taut middle. The other is wiping down his broad, muscled chest as he saunters over. His dark hair has coiled into a bed of damp curls.

It can't be.

It's an illusion; a ghost of a memory:

Of the very first time I saw him…

But then that seductive grin I covet raises on his lips, and I know exactly what he'll say next:

"Honey, I'm home."

I force myself to stammer, "But… How? …"

He falls onto the bed beside me. He yelps when I leap into his arms; and when I pummel him with kisses—

And then with my fists. My laughter turns to sobs, and, finally to the question that needs an answer so that I can believe that all of this is real: "How did you survive?"

"I tell you, doll: Dominic is going to make a mint with those bulletproof tuxes." He shakes his head, awed. "As a precaution, I attached a few more fake-blood packets to the jacket, front and back and in the sleeves, just in case things didn't go as planned."

"Smart thinking! My God! If Oleg had shot you in the head instead—"

"I was more concerned that you were going to shoot *him*, and we wouldn't discover Eagle and Snake's endgame."

I reach into my pocket and pull out the missive that is to go to Cheever. "Now that I don't have to mourn you, I'll send this over to Emma right now for deciphering."

"I know she and the rest of the team are freaking out that you may have gone rogue after my detour… Still, can't it wait?" Jack makes his plea with a long, deep kiss.

I linger in it, reveling in the awe that this one sensation holds a universe of emotions:

Joy. Desire. Pain. Hope.

Bliss.

Then, reluctantly, I disentangle my body from his.

"First things first. This goes to Emma. And then I've got to make Cheever fall in love with me."

Jack laughs so hard that he chokes on his words: "Wow! I never thought I'd hear *that* come out of your mouth."

I pick his shirt off the floor and toss it to him. "And you never will again. But when this is over, we pick up right here, where we left off."

My vow is my kiss to him.

19

Fake Famous

DO YOU HAVE WHAT IT TAKES TO BE "FAKE FAMOUS," THAT IS, *famous for no particular talent other than have others following you on social media?*

You really think so, answer the following questions:

1: WHICH ONE BEST DESCRIBES YOU?
- *I really, really, really DESERVE to be famous.*
- *I'd like to be famous.*
- *I could take or leave being famous.*

2: SAME HERE—BEST ANSWER, PLEASE:
- *I look great in pictures.*
- *I never look my age in photos—and that's a good thing.*
- *Okay, truth be told, I think look passable in pictures.*

(Reality is immaterial.)

· · ·

3: YES, OR NO?

·   *I don't mind checking my SM feeds every five minutes to see how many people like what I post. In fact, I judge my success by likes.*

·   *I don't mind pimping products that are sent at me to hold in pictures.*

·   *I think I can fake out authenticity software.*

·   *To be honest, I don't even know what "authenticity software" is.*

A OR B:

·   *I live close enough to walls that are one bright color to pose in front of them.*

·   *I don't lean up against strange walls because I don't want to get dirty.*

ANSWER KEY:

Any answer that was first, Yes, or A means you will cry yourself to sleep if you fail as a social media influencer.

All other answers mean that you'll lead a much fuller life.

"RISE AND SHINE, SLEEPY HEAD!" I'VE GOTTEN OUT OF MY Candy mask long enough for Miss Delish to slap Grady into consciousness.

He groans. Finally, his eyes fly wide open. Cautiously, he looks down at his feet. Whereas the pillow hasn't moved, his tethers have been removed, and he is no longer gagged.

"Justin confirmed what you told me," I explain. "That you had no knowledge of what covert intel was being posted on your social media feeds. You're free to go."

I don't mention that Justin is no longer among the living. I don't want to freak him out.

"But… So… What am I going to do for the tournament?"

"Can't any of the others in your clown car of an entourage tell you what you're going to cook?" I cock a brow. "Or better yet, why not—oh, I don't know—*wing it*, like any real chef would do?"

"Hey, don't be so mean," he sniffs.

"I'm teasing." I pull the cheat sheet Acme has made for him. "If you need inspiration, the Feds found this on Justin. They didn't think it was important, so they left it."

Grady scans it. "Thank goodness! It's the recipe for my fail-safe beef stew." He chuckles. "That Justin. At least he went out on a high note. Listen to this closing line: 'Stew is a slow-cook meal, so if you burn it, you own it.'"

"We're decoding the real message now," Emma murmurs through my buds.

Grady sighs. "At least it makes more sense than some of the one-liners he's given me in the past."

I perk up. "Oh yeah? Like what?"

Grady rolls his eyes. "Well, a few days back, he had me say, 'Nobody likes hot soup—except in winter. So, enjoy!' When I pointed out to him that it's the middle of summer,' he made up some cockamamie line, like, 'Not in Australia.' Granted, he was right. Still, only sixteen percent of my FaceStaTweet followers are down under! So, like why turn off the other eighty-four percent with cold soup?"

"He must have had his reasons," I reply.

"I'll say!" Emma exclaims—so loud that I must shake my head to get her voice out of it. "The cipher correlates to an incident that took place in Australia when Sydney's electrical grid was taken offline for almost an hour. The government claimed the fault was a software glitch, but in truth it was ransomware that took it down. The Aussies were smart enough to have an alternate current switch."

"Well, at least he didn't leave you in the lurch!" I kiss Grady gently on the cheek. "May the best chef win."

"MA! WHAT THE HECK TOOK YOU SO LONG? I'VE GOT TO BE downstairs in less than a—" Cheever's jaw drops when he sees that it's not Penelope standing at his door, but Candy Murphy in a hot pink ballgown that plunges both in the front and the back while hugging all the right places. "Um…You are *not* my mom…"

I shrug. "No kidding. Want to try a different come-on line, because that one really sucks."

Cheever's cheeks pink up. When he realizes the opportunity that has just been presented to him, he puffs up like a toad. "Sure… As long as Randy isn't around the corner, waiting for someone to say the wrong thing to his honey. I ain't cruisin' for a bruisin'. The braces just came off my sexy-as-shite choppers a week ago."

"Not to worry. We split up—for good."

Cheever's eyes bulge. "Really? He let a sweet piece of hot flesh like you walk away—just like that?"

"There was nothing he could do to stop me. I had my

mind made up that I no longer wanted him as my old man."

"But... why? I mean... you guys look as if you were made for each other, you know? Like, a real-life Ken and Barbie."

I snicker. "You're not hearing me. I said I don't want an old man. Like, you know—old. I like my men as... well, boys." I give him the once-over.

Cheever gulps.

Maybe that was a burp he let loose with.

I sniff the air...

Agh! *A fart.*

That's no way to woo a lady.

But it's a great sign of my ability to intimidate the heck out of him.

I pinch his cheek. "Don't worry, I don't bite."

That puts a leer on his face—

Until I add: "I spank. *Hard.*"

He backs away, frightened.

I purr, "Your mother told me you're a good boy, that you'll do everything I ask."

He nods obediently.

I take the missive he's to say to his followers during his tournament round.

It's not the one Oleg gave me—which, according to Emma, although ComInt was able to break the code, the words presented make absolutely no sense:

RELEASE ROD IN TWELVE

If Cheever had written it for himself, I could imagine

him sniggering before following through on some vulgar act of personal violation while the tournament streams live.

Maybe I should ask him outright. He's so enthralled with Candy that he may blab it right out.

I take a tendril of Candy's long blond wig and wrap it around my finger. In my sweetest little girl voice, I coo, "I don't get it. What does it mean?"

His mouth opens—

But then it snaps shut again. "Oh, no you don't!" He snatches it out of my hand. "You're not stealing it as your own coded message."

"Wait… You know the messages are coded?"

"What do you think I am, some sort of ignoramus?" he sneers. "If this came from Ma, then it also came from the head honcho sponsor. If you go on the air and say it first, I lose my sponsorship money—and my sponsor to boot—*to you*! That ain't gonna happen. My mom would kill me."

He can't be complicit in an act of terrorism. He can go to prison for it.

How do I explain that to him?

"Listen, Cheever, I know you love all the money you're making. It's like a really big high, right? But you've got a bigger high in store for you. Something that will make you proud, that will prove what kind of man you are—"

He roars with laughter. "Wow! Who ever thought that Candy Murphy, queen of the glamping influencers, would be trying to seduce *me*—just some pipsqueak from Hilldale, California?"

"What?…But I'm not—"

"Look, don't think I'm not flattered or anything, but…I

mean, come on. My follower numbers are now *way* bigger than yours! And they're going to stay that way. You're old news, Candy. And no matter how badly you beg to do the no-pants dance with Cheever—no matter how long and hard you beg to do the two-person pushup with this guy, it ain't going to happen! So before you humiliate yourself—"

"Wait a minute! You think I—"

"Cheever, are you going to be much longer? Because if we're not doing this thing..." Mary's voice trails off.

What the heck is my daughter doing here, in Cheever's suite?

In the doorway of Cheever's bedroom, no less.

Mary frowns. "Get rid of her—or I'm leaving. Like, *now.*"

"Mary, please! Stay right there. You promised we'd..." Cheever shoves me toward the front door.

The next thing I know, the door locks behind me.

I bang on it, but he's not answering?

What the hell does Mary think she's doing?

"Oleg is waiting for Candy in his cabin," Emma warns me.

"I can't worry about him now!" I mutter back. "For some crazy reason, Mary is in Cheever's cabin."

"Yikes! Maybe it has something to do with the text she just got. I could tell it made her livid because she took off like a shot."

"Who was if from? Jack? Ryan?" I ask.

"No…" Emma sighs. "You know, the security of her cell isn't yet up to Acme level. I'd have to hack it…"

"I'll pretend I didn't hear that," I assure her.

"Okay…well… In the meantime, you should go babysit Oleg. He's already suspicious since you… um…beat him up."

She's right. He likes things rough, but I may have gone too far. "Okay, Candy is headed there now. Tell me, is Mary at least wearing eyes and ears?"

"Unfortunately, no."

"Then at the very least you can monitor her in case… in case…"

In case Cheever physically attacks her.

The words stick in my throat. Finally, I'm able to croak: "Please keep Jack apprised to Mary's situation, in case she needs back-up."

"Not Evan?"

The question makes me flinch. "His emotions may be too raw for whatever she's got in mind. Remember, despite his clearance for this mission, he's still a civilian. That opens him up to liability we don't have."

"I guess you're right. Except that Jack…Well, never mind."

"Jack is what, Emma? Come out with it already."

"He's got his hands full too. Something big is going down! But I swear to you, Donna! I won't let anything happen to Mary. After we found out about Penelope's ties to Oleg, we've had Cheever's cabin and devices bugged, remember?"

Relief washes over me. "Ah, right! Thanks for reminding me."

"Gotta go! ComInt has just walked in with an encryption that may blow this thing wide open!"

As long as I don't blow us all sky high.

"YOU TOOK YOUR SWEET TIME." OLEG YANKS ME INTO HIS suite.

I jerk my hand away. "I had a couple of deliveries to make, remember?"

He folds his arms in front of his chest. "And?"

"Despite Justin's extermination, Grady is onboard. Justin had already given him his talking points."

Oleg's scowl holds firm, but his nod gives away his relief.

"And Cheever is my very willing bitch," I proclaim. "He knows what to say verbatim."

Oleg shrugs. "Ah, young love. Or should I say lust?" He eyes me longingly. "You're wasted as an influencer. I like you better as my enforcer."

I run my finger along his jaw. "That makes two of us."

He tenses. He thinks I'm going to slap him.

Instead I pat his cheek lovingly. "After we get off this cruise from hell, we'll kiss and make up."

He pulls me close for a kiss now.

When our mouths meet, I resist the urge to put my arms around his neck—if only to snap it.

The knock on the door makes me glad I kept my cool. I look him over. "Are you expecting company?"

"Just the last piece of the intricate puzzle I've devised." He turns to the door and barks: "Come in."

And I find myself face to face with the dynamic dance duo of Eric and Erica.

Well what do you know…

AS THE QUOTE-UNQUOTE DYNAMIC DANCE TEAM OF ERIC AND Erica stroll through the front door, I mutter loud enough for them to hear: "About damn time."

Erica frowns. "Hi to you too."

Shit…

Does that mean we're supposed to know each other?

On the other hand, Eric laughs. He's intrigued.

So much so that he thinks nothing of getting in my face to say, "We meet…finally." He loses his grin for a moment, if only to sound sincere when he adds, "Sorry to hear that Randy bit the dust." But the million-watt smile is back in a nanosecond as he adds: "I guess you'll be looking for a new partner to share your tent, eh?"

I place a hand on his chest. "Why? Do you want to apply for the gig?"

"Tempt me," he teases.

I glance behind him to see how Erica is taking his blatant flirtation. Since she's occupied chewing up Oleg's face, I guess she's fine and dandy about it.

My, my, this is an incestuous clique.

"It must be *so, so hard*"—I linger on that last word— "what with all the lifting and bending you dancers must do." I roll my eyes in Erica's direction. "Not that she's a heifer or anything."

She breaks her lip lock on Oleg long enough to shoot me a dirty look.

"Let's just say it keeps me flexible." To prove it he bends me back as he kisses me—

If that's what he wants to call it. At the very least, his tongue is slithering around my mouth.

I choke back the bile climbing up my throat.

He pulls away—

That is, he is pulled away—

By Oleg. "Now that we've said our hello's, let's get down to business." Oleg puts his arm around my waist.

Erica's eyes narrow to slits, whereas Eric shrugs. "Yeah, sure." This pissing contest is over, leaving his shoes soaked.

"Candy has taken over the running of the gamer brat and the idiot chef," Oleg explains. "They've got their marching orders, so we're in play."

"You're pulling her out of the field?" Erica gives me the stink-eye.

"She's earned it. She lured Jack Craig out of hiding." Oleg shrugs. "He's been exterminated. And now that Randy is no longer with us—or Justin—she's won their assets' trust."

"It's easy enough to do when all it takes is spreading your legs," Erica huffs.

I shake my head. "Isn't that the pot calling the kettle black?"

"More like me calling you a whore," Erica retorts.

Oleg looks down at this watch. "We don't have time for your pouting, Erica. If you remember, we are down several operatives. Lyle is currently being interrogated by the FBI, and the Lóngs have disappeared. I assume they saw the writing on the wall when I told them you were to be the Dance category winners and have made good on their threats to go back to the MSS."

"Well, good riddance," Erica exclaims. "And we're to be the overall winners, too, as promised—am I right?"

Oleg waves away the supposition. "Yes, a superlative payday is in your future—if all goes as planned. After the brat and the chef follow through with their acts, you're in play. So you'd better get moving."

Erica leaps up, ecstatic. "If we're successful, Orel i Zmeya will forever be known as the terrorists who brought the United States' energy grid to its knees!"

Finally, I know the game plan.

Australia was just a test.

But how will Eagle and Snake do it?

Oleg reaches down behind the desk. "All fans and VIPs have their gift cell phones—an appropriate party favor, eh?" He chuckles. "And these commemorative cells have already sold out on FaceStaTweet. The Lifestyle category will be first. That imbecile, Dominic, is leading with likes and followers. No problem. We'll divert the current created by his followers' votes into a holding cable so that its surge is timed to the big finale."

"But how is it possible to take down the whole energy grid, from here on some cruise liner in Chesapeake Bay?" I ask.

"Where have you been, hiding under a rock?" Erica sniggers. "Oh, yeah—in the woods, taking your stupid glam shots. Well, since Oleg has somehow neglected to bring you up to speed, here's the flash card version." She leans in as if divulging a secret. "The question is no longer how it will happen, but who will have the honor of doing it first. The Russians, Chinese, North Koreans, and Iranians are all vying for the crown. But we're going to beat them to it! And not just by debilitating a transponder or two, like the few lone wolf attacks by white supremacists and Bugaloos."

"Then, how, exactly?" I ask.

"The whole Eastern Seaboard—fifteen states and the District of Columbia—are serviced by one grid," Eric pipes up. "All that's needed is to take ten percent of its generators offline—that is, hack then command the generators' industrial control systems to close their circuit breakers—and ninety-three million people—including DC—are in the dark."

"In the meantime, we divert the energy to blow up the closest nuclear plant." Erica points out the suite's vast deck:

The Prince Charles is now docked outside a nuclear facility—

Two, in fact.

"Bingo," Ryan murmurs into my ear. "Those are the Calvert Cliffs Nuclear Power plants.

"Now, our goal is to find Eagle and Snake's energy holding cable," Jack adds, "so that we can cut the surge that it plans to initiate from the ship."

"On it," Arnie mutters.

But how can he do this—let alone Abu—when they've got to be on stage as their influencer personas?

"Subsequent surges will come from Food, Gaming, and of course yours, Dance" —he nods toward Erica and Eric—

"which is now yours for the taking since I took care of the contestant who was wiping the floor with you: LOL Pasadena."

Thank you, Oleg, for confirming another reason I should guarantee your delivery to a dark place from which you will never return. RIP Joe the Poser…

Glaring at Erica, I add: "And you can thank me for encouraging Joe the Poser to jump ship—literally."

"You see? Another problem solved—so that you can win more easily!" Oleg chides the dancers. "No one can say Candy isn't a team player."

From Erica's glower, I'm sure she has a few choice names for me—none of which is that one.

Eagle and Snake's leader looks from one dancer to the other. "I assume you have your props ready?"

They nod.

What props? And what do they have to do with the power surge?

"Good. Then we'd better head down to the auditorium," Oleg commands. But as I turn to go, he holds firm to my arm. "Candy, we have a bit of a dilemma."

Eric and Erica stop to listen.

"FaceStaTweet seems to have lost yet another contestant: the food influencer, Miss Delish."

The dancers stare at me. I shrug. "Sadly, she did something stupid."

"What was that, exactly?" Oleg asks.

"She walked in on me and Grady as we were discussing his messaging. I assume you're just as upset as me that she drowned. Not that her body will be found anytime soon."

Eric guffaws. "Let me guess: she fell overboard—with a little encouragement from you."

"Wrong," I reply. "It happened in the bathtub. No one can hold their breath for five minutes, although she tried her best."

Oleg smirks, "You see? I don't know what I'd do without my dear Candy."

Too bad. He's about to find out.

20

Live Stream

WHETHER THE MEDIUM IS SOCIAL MEDIA OR A TELEVISION OR cable network, when video or audio is produced in the moment, it is called "live streaming."

The good thing about live streaming: you can promote it in advance, and thusly grow your audience.

Another good thing about live streaming: it also allows for audience interaction.

Word of warning: anything can and will go wrong. For example, if you or your guest say something that ends up shocking your viewers, then, as Ricky Ricardo invariably told Lucy, "You got some 'splaining to do!"

Solution: record in advance and leave the faux pas on the cutting room floor.

~

OLEG, ERIC, ERICA AND I ENTER THE ONE ELEVATOR FROM THE VIP floors to the ballroom on the top deck. But there is yet another floor above Oleg's: the Presidential deck.

When it opens I try hard not to keep from gasping. Relief roils through me when I realize that it's not Lee and the soccer team getting in the elevator but Dominic and his entourage. They think nothing of cramming in, forcing us all the way to the back.

Oleg says nothing but he seethes until, finally, the doors open, expelling Dominic and his loud crowd.

"What a clown," Oleg mutters.

Eric and Erica laugh raucously as they head toward the stage.

Spotlights throughout the room roam over the crowd of fans whose frenzied cheers greet each contestant as they take their places in the boxes designated for their category.

Each box is backlit in the category's designated color. For Lifestyle, it's red. For Food, it is blue. The gamers' box is orange, whereas the dancers are in the green box.

Gracing the stage is a full-story high statue lined in gold—a duplicate of the trophy to go to the winner.

Eric and Erica take their places in the green box beside the only two competing influencers who hadn't been eliminated, physically, that is: The Lóng Twins, and Abu.

Oleg leads me to the VIP box reserved specifically for him. He too notices the Lóng Twins. "They dare to compete instead of mourn their parents?"

I snort. "If you had Ming and Hu as so-called parents, wouldn't you be celebrating your independence from those two sadists?"

He chortles, "I suppose you're right. Although I assume you'll be no less a taskmaster to them."

"What do you mean?" I ask.

"You're to add little Genghis and Guang to your roster for assets." To make his point that I have no say in his decision, he clenches my thigh tightly.

Holding back my tears of pain, I nod nonchalantly. "Expect to pay a high price."

"I understand. They are a wily duo."

I look him in the eye. "No. I meant for bruising me."

He smirks. "I'd expect so."

Will they have cattle prods at the dark site where he'll end up? I hope so.

If not, I'll be sure to send one, with my compliments.

AS ERICA PREDICTED, DOMINIC EASILY WALKS AWAY WITH THE highest tally of Best Lifestyle Influencer.

It helped that Lyle Greenwich is in police custody, and thus out of the running.

Mina Concha seems relieved that that she isn't the winner. Frankly, that raises her value in my eyes. As much as I know she loves sharing her posts with others, she wants to do it her way: no pressure, just fun.

Good for her.

Despite losing out to him, Sammy French and Alana Partain think nothing of smothering Dominic in kisses. But then things get rough. First Alana shoves Sammy—

Who slaps her.

Soon they are pulling each other's hair, until they fall on the floor, slapping and grappling.

Dominic walks away, into the arms of his adoring entourage, who takes him around to shake hands with his fans.

When the women realize that no one is watching, they help each other to their feet.

All you've got to know is everything is show biz…

And that's when I notice the red glass rod on a pedestal at the front of the stage.

Dominic goes to it, takes it in hand, and then walks to the stage's centerpiece: a two-story aluminum column of the FaceStaTweet trophy. Just like the trophy, the company's logo is cut out vertically at two-foot intervals throughout the statue.

When Dominic taps it with the rod, an electrical charge surges through the trophy, lighting it a deep scarlet hue.

The glow, though dim, pulsates continually.

Acme has yet to break the cable.

THE CHEFS ARE UP NEXT. IT'S A HOT CONTEST, SINCE ALL HAVE large followings. Despite wonderful offerings by Stewie (a chicken and rice stew), Sweet Meats (a pulled pork sandwich), and Fake It or Bake it (using macaroni and cheese with porcini mushrooms and prosciutto for a casserole), they don't look as elegant or mouthwatering as Grady's lobster Thermador—

A recipe he stole from the Prince Charles's chef. Talk about cutting corners!

When Grady taps his rod to the humongous trophy, the red glow changes to a bright sky blue. The trophy pulsates brighter and even faster as the energy surges through it.

In his victory speech, Grady delivers the password sentence.

Oleg checks an app on his cell. He frowns.

He gives me a sidelong glance.

I keep my eyes straight ahead and Candy's renowned pout on my lips.

In time, he also shifts his gaze to the stage. But I feel a chill growing between us.

Oleg suspects that something isn't right.

THE GAMERS ARE UP NEXT.

Unlike the other categories where the contestants presented their videos one after another—with the leading influencer going last—the gamers are strictly playing each other in a private match of *Tower of Power*. The five contestants take their places in the large captain's chairs that sit in front of wall-sized monitors throughout the stage. Tremor, Fantasy Fling, and Detonator all have great followings. Their fans who are in attendance scream their names, along with ecstatic encouragement.

But one by one they are knocked out of the game, leaving Arnie and Cheever neck and neck—

Until Arnie's numbers start disappearing.

Arnie jumps up from his chair. "What the hell?"

As his avatar dissolves from the screen, he storms off the stage, screaming, "This is bogus, dudes!"

Cheever stands up and takes a bow. "Now, before I torch the trophy with my own personal Cheever Fever, I've got a very special treat for my followers."

The crowd grows silent, anticipating what's up his sleeve.

"You remember that very hot lady whose video swept SnapCrap? Well, she promised me that if I won, she'd be my guest. So, in a FaceStaTweet exclusive—to which I know you'll all show your appreciation with double and triple likes—you're about hear something about *this* Mary that will blow your mind"—Cheever winks broadly—"as opposed to your—"

The song *Oh Yeah* drowns him out as Mary walks onto the stage and takes a bow.

Oh. My. Gawd.

What the heck is she up to?

The Jumbotron behind the stage shows Mary and Cheever sitting side by side, just as they do now, on stage. However it isn't a live feed, but a recorded video:

MARY:

You were the one who created the fakenude of me, am I right, Cheever?

As in real life, in the recorded video Cheever's mouth drops open. The recording continues:

CHEEVER:

Wow! So you found me out! Okay, yeah, I created it—as payback for all the times you turned me down when we carpooled to school.

MARY:

Seriously, Cheever, how often do I have tell you that you aren't my type?

CHEEVER:

(snickers:)

I don't take no for an answer—even if I create a fake of you getting what you deserve!

MARY:

Cheever, you do know that what you did—creating a fakenude, and then posting it so that it can be seen all over the world—is a Federal offense, right?

CHEEVER:

Big whoop! Hey, I'm famous now! I'm immune to eating the crap that normal people eat—especially when they break laws. So go cry to your mama, little girl.
(He pauses, then smirks):
That very hot mama of yours, who may find herself in one of my porn flicks too.

MARY:

(tears in her eyes:)
You wouldn't dare!

CHEEVER:

I'll tell you what. If I lose, I won't do it. Scout's honor.

MARY:
You've never been a scout.

CHEEVER:
That's beside the point. What I'm telling you is that I'll leave your hot mama out of it.

MARY:
But…what if you win?

CHEEVER:
Then you come onstage with me, and act all in awe of me —you know, 'coz I'm a big shot and can have any girl I want anyway, just for the asking—and …

The screen goes blank.

Mary stands up. "You heard it, folks. Cheever Bing admitted to committing a felony offense that deals with pornography with a minor. He also admitted to being a creep who will use and abuse anyone he wants, including you, his followers. And Cheever thinks he's now too rich and too powerful for you to touch! That he can buy his way out of any situation. What do you say to that?"

The crowd's boos start as a low rumble but soon grow into a roar. They pelt him with their new FaceStaTweet cell phones as he runs to the exit.

That's my girl.

Eyes weighted in suspicion, Oleg stares at me.

Over the speaker, an announcer says: "Since the leading contestant in the gaming category has broken several of FaceStaTweet's governing rules and regulations —as well as a Federal law—he is banned from participating in this competition. Additionally, he is now banned from FaceStaTweet."

The crowd is delirious with excitement.

"By default, the winner of the Game Streaming category is 'Locked and Loaded with Arnie.'"

"*Wahooooo!*" Arnie grabs the rod from Cheever and leaps up onto the stage. When he touches the pole to the statue, its glow turns orange. It pulsates so quickly that sparks shower the stage.

That cannot be good…

"With no further ado, we move on to our last tournament category: Dance! There are three contestants who have made it to the finals. Please welcome the first contender—the Sleek Sikh…"

OLEG GLARES AT ME. "YOUR LITTLE PIG NEVER GAVE THE passcode."

"I'm sure FaceStaTweet cut off his mic," I counter. "He was too much of a liability."

"*It has to be given!*" Oleg insists. "You must deliver it to Eric and Erica. Tell them to incorporate it in their closing remarks."

"Didn't you already give them a specific passcode?" I'm spit-balling here.

Oleg's pause is long enough for me to know I'm right. He thinks he can cover up his tell by snarling, "His needs to be spoken as well."

"But they've left the box! They are getting ready to start their routine. I don't know how to get backstage—"

"That door, there. It takes you under the stage and to the other side, where they are waiting to go on." He points to a door immediately behind us. "Do it now. *Or else.*" He holds my wrist so tightly it feels as if it's breaking.

Thank God he can't hear how my heart bangs against my chest.

I force myself to meet his stare. "Or else what?"

"Don't force my hand, Mrs. Murphy. I am still the head of *Orel i Zmeya.* And despite my obvious attraction to you, I always put business ahead of pleasure. Should this mission go wrong, someone will take the blame—and it won't be me."

Applause explodes around us. Abu has finished his act. He turns to the Jumbotron to see if he has enough points to beat the leads: Erica and Eric.

But no, he hasn't.

Still, he gives a gracious bow to the crowd before trotting off.

The Lóng Twins run onto the stage. The crowd finds their joy infectious. When they begin their synchronized hip-hop routine, to Pharrell William's *Happy,* the crowd's thunderous applause goes into overdrive.

I pull away from Oleg.

Despite his smile, he dismisses me by turning his back.

I GO THROUGH THE DOOR, ONLY TO FIND THAT THERE IS BARELY light in the narrow corridor beyond it.

This cannot be the way.

I go back the few steps I came—

Only to find the door locked.

I bang on it.

Either Oleg doesn't hear, or he's ignoring me.

My guess is the latter.

There is nothing I can do but to keep moving forward.

Using my cellphone as a flashlight, I proceed slowly. I can tell the passageway is dropping below the auditorium floor. It is also curving toward the center near the stage, so I guess Oleg was right about where I'd end up—

Ouch! Or not, considering I've just stumbled against a staircase.

As I make my way up, I hear applause. I guess the Lóng Twins did a wonderful job with their routine. Good! I hope they win the dance category trophy from Eric and Erica.

Frankly, I hope they end up winning the tournament.

By the time I reach the top step, the auditorium crowd is delirious.

Maybe I got my wish after all.

Well, that, and that we all make it off this boat alive.

SHITE! I JUST HIT MY HEAD ON THE CEILING!

How did that happen?...

I feel around until I find a latch. I slide it to one side—

Light fills the passageway. I pull myself up—

To find I'm standing on the stage.

In the metal trophy statue, to be exact.

It is pulsating, as if it holds a million strobe lights, all green.

I touch the statue's side:

Yee-ouch! It shocked me!

I look around. There isn't an exit door onto the stage.

What the…

Oh… no.

I squat down and pull on the trap door, but it won't open. I do the same but now with both hands—

But it still won't budge.

By now, Eric and Erica have walked onto the stage. I hit the statue with my fist to get their attention, ignoring the sharp jolts that run through me every time I touch its smooth metal wall. Erica sees me through one of the logo cut-outs because she looks straight at me, guffaws, then taps her nose with her middle finger.

Same to you, bitch.

The fact that I'm here—on the inside of this metal column, with no way out—

I find a logo cut-out that faces Oleg's box.

When he realizes he is being watched, he grins back at me.

He knew this would happen.

He sent me here to die.

The song that they've chosen is totally old school: Donna Summer's *I Feel Good.*

The dance pair bumps. They grind. They do all the disco moves from *Boogie Nights.*

And while they do this, I bang on the walls with my fist. I get on my knees and claw around the trap door, hoping I can pry it open.

I scream at the top of my lungs.

I pray they don't win, so that I'm not electrocuted.

Then the music ends and the crowd roars with adulation. They clap as if two hundred people are one—three times in a row, followed by two claps—as they chant *Erica! Eric! Erica! Eric!*

The next minute is the longest in my life. I count down the seconds, standing perfectly still within what will soon be my aluminum casket.

Then the screaming starts.

Eric and Erica have won.

I stay very still, in the very center of the statue. I wonder how long it will take before the static surrounds me; how many seconds I have before it fills my lungs—

Before it stops my heart.

When I crumple to the ground, will I burn to a crisp?

Will my body be found? Even so, will it be singed beyond recognition?

Or will I be just a pile of ashes?

I see them now, walking over to the statue. Each holds a green pole: they tap them together, acknowledging their victory. Then they tap the statute—

And I brace for the surge—

For the world to light up—

And then to go…

Dark.

Nothing.

I open my eyes. Darkness surrounds me.

And the shouts start: "What's happening?" and "Where are the lights?"

Consternation rocks the ballroom, a torrent of surprise, roiled with concern, hazed in disappointment.

Not me. I am elated.

I am alive.

Finally, the auditorium's lights go on again.

And then the screaming starts.

And the wailing.

I look out one of the cutouts facing the stage.

Eric and Erica lie on the floor.

At least, I presume it is them. I can't be sure because the bodies are no more than blackened carcasses.

I move to the other side of the statue, to find Oleg.

While others rush toward the stage, he heads out of his private box.

I hear a tap coming from the trap door.

I pound it with my heel. "Open up! I'm in here!"

I'm not surprised when it opens, and Jack is standing there. "Are you going to stay in here all evening? This tug has finally docked. Time to abandon ship!"

"I've never heard a sweeter phrase," I exclaim.

JACK INSISTS THAT WE WAIT UNTIL WE'RE BACK IN HIS SUITE with our mission team before answering any questions.

I don't mind keeping mute. I feel as if I have a new lease on life. All five senses are in overdrive. The smell of the bay bombards my nostrils. The Easter-egg blue sky makes me blink. I love the moist heat of the sun on my skin as we walk from an outer deck to the quickest elevator bank to take us to the others.

The door opens on the first knock. The next thing I know, I am in the center of a group hug.

I've never been so happy to be alive.

Which leads to my very first question: "Why aren't I dead?"

"You can thank Mary and Evan for that," Jack replies.

"How? Why?" I ask.

"I think we should start at the beginning." Ryan's voice comes in through the cell's speaker. "The game plan was for the Eastern Seaboard to go dark, at which point Oleg was going to collect a several-billion-dollar ransom from the US government before removing the trojan that knocked it out."

"The ridicule toward our country would have been worth another billion, at least," Jack adds.

"How was Oleg going to carry off his plan?" I ask.

"He released malware in the nuclear generator's industrial control system—its ICS. In the meantime, he diverted some of the energy to a holding grid set up for Eagle and Snake, which he was going to sell to terrorist groups, both stateside and foreign. The FaceStaTweet event guaranteed a big pull on the grid. Each time the millions of FaceStaTweet account holders voted across its whole platform during the tournament meant yet another surge from the closest energy source."

"It's why the Prince Charles was anchored so close to the Calvert Cliffs Nuclear Plant," I reason.

"Exactly," Ryan confirms.

I turn to Evan. "How did you stop the steal?"

"BlackTech has developed a software program that specifically searches and destroys ransomware," he explains. "But before we could upload it, Eagle and Snake's had already started diverting energy. Its holding grid's gauge was FaceStaTweet's tournament tower."

"Which is why, when I was stuck in the tower, I might have died," I murmur.

"And the metal corridor blocked my warnings not to continue through the underground corridor but to instead stay put until we could come get you," Emma adds.

"Which brings me back to my original question: why didn't I die?"

"Several reasons," Jack continues. "For one, you stayed away from the metal sides of the column. For another, you're wearing rubber-soled shoes. And the final reason: Evan's software stopped the energy diversion in the nick of time."

"And yet, Eric and Erica were electrocuted when their rods touched the statue," I point out.

Whereas, by sheer luck, I avoided that fate.

"According to the notes Oleg made on his cell, he was livid at the idea of paying such exorbitant bonuses to his operatives. It didn't matter to him if they got electrocuted, or whether some innocent contestant was the victim. The effect on the ship's audience and the world news would have been the same: adding another layer of horror to Eagle and Snake's act of terrorism. Either way, it was a win-win. To Oleg's mind, operatives—especially those who keep upping the ante—are easily replaceable. To that end, he was appreciative that Candy took care of Penelope for him, as well as Justin."

"He made a similar promise to me. I guess that his promise to take me with him would have been a death sentence." I shudder. "Now that the ship has docked, I assume he's gotten away?"

Mary grins. "Not quite. I was with Dominic's posse when they got on the elevator with you and Oleg. The crush allowed me to stand directly behind him. I planted a GPS microdot on his jacket. A limo driver was holding up a sign that said REX. He got into that car."

"Rex is French for 'king,'" I retort. "He certainly has a high opinion of himself."

"The FBI will be the best reality check on his ego. Its agents raided his safe house. He's in custody now." She holds up her hand for a high five, which I slap. "Mario called me a chip off the old block."

"I'm not that old," I mutter.

"That's what I told him. He told me I'm too loyal—to you."

"Ah? Did he now?" *Grrrrr…*

"I told him he's right. My loyalties lie with my family, first and foremost. Always and forever."

Like Mario said: a chip off the block.

Make that a sweet, gorgeous, kick-ass, doesn't-look-her-age block.

21

Brand Advocate

IF YOU'RE GOING TO GO—AND STAY—ON SOCIAL MEDIA, you're going to need a few brand advocates.

Who are they, you ask?

Ideally, they are people who believe in your message—your vision—who freely and eagerly post encouraging messages and reviews about you, your product, or your brand. Doing so encourages others' awareness of you. They too will be curious as to who you are, and why so many people are saying such wonderful things about you.

It's a form of word-of-mouth marketing.

Think back to the days before social media, when your inspiring words and generous deeds were enthusiastically relayed by friends, family, and perhaps a few complete strangers for whom you'd done a kindness or two.

But instead, this person-to-person conversation—about little ol' you—is taking place online, in several places via numerous posts, and thus multiplying the awareness to your actions! Pretty cool, right?

Then again, the same could happen if someone catches you being cruel or catty and puts it up on some social media platform. In a matter of moments, your reputation as an upstanding citizen could be shredded by the claws of indignation; in the jaws from which angry soundbites are spewed.

The solution: I wish I could say there is a time machine to take us back to the days before social media.

Alas, there isn't. We must make do with the choices offered in the here and now.

Ergo, since the role of saint doesn't necessarily come naturally to you, I suggest you zip your lips and don't go out without a disguise.

Or pray for a giant meteor to take Earth back to the Stone Age.

(I wouldn't mind starting over. How about you?)

LEE TOSSES ME AN APPLE, THEN SITS DOWN BESIDE ME. "I guess your frenemy will soon be the mean mom-queen bee in some Federal penitentiary to be designated sometime soon." Now that FaceStaTweet has gone dark and the few influencers left are stranded to find their own way home, he has graciously allowed our mission team to hitch a ride on his private plane.

I appreciate the fruit. However, I am not as tempted to rise to his bait on Penelope. "Frankly, I feel sorry for her. At least when she ruled the school she was anchored to some form of reality, as cockeyed as it was. Her whole world is—*was*—Hilldale. Her role as a wife, mother, and social maven was clearly defined. Sadly, her time on that reality show—*Housewives of Hilldale*—really went to her head. And when she and Peter split up, I think she became scared." I nibble on the apple. Just knowing what's ahead for her is enough to make me lose my appetite.

Lee glances around. Noting how close we are to Trisha and Janie, he leans in. I do the same. "Surely any intel she can give them on Oleg will help to cut a few years off her sentence. So will returning Cheever's ill-gotten sponsorship payments."

"She'll talk all right. She's not cut out for prison life. Although I fear Cheever would thrive in any environment, including prison. He'll do anything—including something bad—for notoriety. His stint as an influencer proved that."

Jack sits down on the other side of me. "I'm not interrupting anything, am I?"

With a straight face, Lee replies, "Other than yet another attempt at my asking your wife to run away with me, nah. And yet again, she has turned me down."

"You'd think you'd have learned your lesson by now," Jack replies coolly.

More like an icy Alaskan cold front.

I stand up. "Now boys, if you can't play nice, I prefer you not play at all. This isn't a game. I am not the trophy."

I look from Jack to Lee and back again.

Lee nods first. He holds out his hand to Jack, who takes it—

And squeezes it until Lee grunts, "What am I supposed to say, now? 'Uncle?'"

I shake my head. "Work it out, boys, before we land. Otherwise, the team dinner that Janie and Trisha have been talking about since they left the ship will be cancelled. And you"—I point to Jack—"and you"—I turn to Lee—"will have to explain why."

Lee stands up. "I extend an olive branch, Jack. I am truly sorry—that you found the perfect woman before I had a chance to sweep her off her feet."

"Ah! Well, thanks for that half-ass albeit heartfelt apology, Lee." Jack tips his imaginary hat at our host. "And I'm sorry that all your money and great looks and charm hasn't allowed you to steal her away from me. But as they say: there are other fish in the sea—"

"I say, sirs!" Dominic is leaning against the wall.

Egad! How long has he been there?

From the smirk on his face, I'd say long enough. To prove me right, he adds: "Per our imperious chieftain, it is time to halt your quibbling over the fair damsel and come into the conference room. News awaits." Dominic takes my arm and leads the way.

Duly chastised, Lee and Jack follow us in.

ARNIE AND ABU ARE ALREADY SEATED. THEY NOD TO US.

"About damn time," Ryan grumbles. "DNI Branham doesn't like to be kept waiting."

Jack shoots Lee a dirty look. "Sorry chief. Donna didn't want to be rude and excuse herself from our host's scintillating conversation."

Whereas Lee gives him a dirty look, that earns him a kick him under the table—from me.

"What's up boss?" I purr sweetly.

"I'm happy to report that the SD Card is already doing its job," Ryan announces.

"Better late than never," Marcus adds gruffly. "And thanks to Mary's quick thinking, Oleg has been taken to a secure location, where he'll be interrogated about the missions of Eagle and Snake. I assume he'll be detained for a very long time."

I'm fine with that.

"Now, for some disappointing news."

Jack's smile disappears, as does mine. Like me, he's bracing himself for what we're about to hear:

"Before FaceStaTweet came back online, it scrubbed its site of Eagle and Snake's account, which means that all its messages to and from its operatives are gone with the wind," Branham says. "This way they can just say, 'We're sorry as sorry can be that we didn't catch it in time, but we took off the bad stuff the moment we became aware of it.' They're worried investors will back off otherwise."

Aw, heck! I forgot to mention to Ryan that it might happen, leaving us with no intel to analyze.

I know neither Ryan nor Marcus can see me throw up my hands, but I do it anyway. "Doesn't FaceStaTweet understand that we need to analyze the information to catch the bad guys?"

"It's covering its ass," Branham replies.

"So, why doesn't the government put its foot on FaceStaTweet's neck to retrieve the intel? It has the power to do so," Jack insists.

"FaceStaTweet is using Section 230 in Title 47 of the United States Code of the Communications Decency Act to claim, and I quote, 'it must remove materials illegal on a Federal level,'" explains Ryan.

Jack groans. "In other words, despite ComInt's success in breaking its cipher, we don't know which accounts belonged to its operatives?"

"I'm afraid not," Branham admits. "To top it off, FaceStaTweet's executive board has resigned en masse. No one wants their fingerprints on this fiasco."

Arnie is giggling.

"What's so funny?" Abu asks.

"It was Emma's idea," Arnie explains. "Go ahead and tell them, Em."

"Our friend the Mad Hacker has talked her pals who run an organization called 'Who Wrote What When and Where' into releasing their daily cache of FaceStaTweet's posts to us. It's a digital record of every account's posts since the platform launched."

"How and why would they create such a thing?" Dominic asks.

"It's what nerds do," Emma explains. "Creating an archive of every public account on every social media platform is a mission that the organization feels is needed. And, I guess when you believe in something and you have time on your hands, you follow through. Sort of like the folks who created SETI—you know, the people who listen for alien contact from outer space?"

"As always, the Mad Hacker knows where to go to find the goods," I declare.

Love that gal.

∾

DESPITE PRODS FROM EVAN AND MARY—AND CERTAINLY from the soccer team—to join them, Jeff is holed up in a row by himself. Even the only other boy on the plane—Genghis, who, with Guang, are coming back to Los Angeles with Jody—couldn't get him out of his doldrums.

It's my turn to try.

I walk over with a tray holding two plates of roast beef sandwiches and German potato salad, and two cans of Ginger Ale: his favorite lunch. "Mind if I join you?"

Jeff shrugs.

I sit down. "Grab a plate." I nod toward the tray.

He does as I ask, but he doesn't dig in.

"Tell me what's wrong," I ask.

He frowns. "I'm thinking about…well about Cheever." He turns so that we're eye to eye. "I hate the thought of what he did to Mary."

"Why do you think he's always been so cruel?" I ask.

"Because his mother allows him to keep doing that sort of stuff," Jeff retorts. "So, it's her fault, not his!"

"Yes, Mrs. Bing has to take some of the blame. She also makes mistakes of her own—and now has broken the law as well. As a legal adult, the consequences will be severe. But Jeff, at what point in Cheever's life will he begin to question his mother's judgement?"

"He's… well, he's Cheever. He's not used to anyone telling him no. But you're right." Jeff's voice is so soft that I can barely hear what he says next: "Mom, tell me the truth: what's going to happen to Cheever?"

I sigh. "He broke a Federal law. Actions come with consequences."

"It was a stupid thing. I mean, he's always done stupid things. But he's just a kid!" Jeff points out.

"Yes…and no," I counter. "He was willing to say anything to keep viewers. He'll have to pay the price. More to the point, when will he finally take responsibility for his own actions?"

Jeff frowns. "He couldn't help himself. He loves the power he wielded as an influencer."

"Even so, there are lots of people who are powerful— even others who have large followings on silly things like FaceStaTweet. Still, they wouldn't think of ruining someone else's life just to increase their viewership."

Jeff nods stoically. "He'll lose any friends he had."

I grimace. "Besides Morton and you, who else hangs with him?"

"Frankly, no one. And we've only hung in there because of all the years we've carpooled with him. Now that he'll no longer be allowed to be on the internet, I guess all his followers will drop him too. It's sad."

"You're right. He'll need friends now more than ever," I point out.

"Are you saying you won't mind if I write him, wherever he ends up?"

"Frankly, I'd be very disappointed if you didn't. Everyone makes mistakes. And if he's willing to own up to them, it's the best way to honor his effort."

He takes a bite of his sandwich and chews thoughtfully. After he swallows, he says, "I'll write him every week for a year. That way, he won't feel so alone."

"You're a good friend," I say.

"Mom… What if Cheever never changes?"

"Then you have no obligation to him. You will have done your best to be his friend."

Then it will be up to Cheever to prove that he deserves Jeff's friendship.

$$\sim$$

WITH THEIR HEADS TOGETHER, MARY AND EVAN ARE giggling.

Just like old times.

Thank goodness.

When they realize I'm curious as to what has them in stitches, their faces go blank.

They aren't getting off that easy.

I sit down beside them. "What's so funny?"

Evan shrugs. "You may not find it funny at all."

"Try me."

They glance at each other. Finally, Mary says, "We were remembering the look on your face when you thought Dad had died."

"*Excuse me*? Somehow you find that laughable?"

"Um...well... I guess you're right. You didn't really know that he was in one of Dominic's bulletproof tuxes."

"In hindsight, it seems as if we should all be laughing out of relief. We all survived this mission." To prove my point, I try to laugh.

But I can't.

Instead, I cry.

Hard.

So hard that Evan is too stunned to do anything, to say anything.

Concerned but not knowing what else to do, he moves off the sofa.

He's looking for Jack, I guess.

He's right. Jack would know what to do to make me stop reliving my worst nightmare.

Mary knows what to do too: she puts her arms around me.

She shushes me. She doesn't let go.

Not even after the last tear has fallen.

Even then, it takes her a while to say: "I don't know how you do it."

"Sometimes, I don't know how I do it either," I admit. "But…that doesn't stop me from doing what I must."

"It almost did tonight."

"Yes." I sigh. "But I got over it…in time."

Just in the nick of time.

"I never heard anyone speak to Ryan the way you did, when you told him you weren't going to play Candy!" She shivers.

I chuckle. "Ryan isn't the all-powerful Wizard of Oz. Sometimes I have to play Dorothy and remind him of that. All's well that ends well." I stroke her cheek. "By the way, you handled the news about the DeepNude brilliantly."

"Thanks." Still astounded, Mary shakes her head. "But can you believe it was Cheever? That little son of a—"

"Yes, I can believe it. And yes, he is a …" I stop. No matter what epitaphs I throw at him, nothing will change him.

Well, prison will give it a good shot, even if it's a juvenile detention facility.

If the Feds decide to try him as an adult, it may be a whole different matter.

So instead, I shrug. "In the meantime, you'll get to take your place as class valedictorian after all."

Mary smiles. "I worked hard all year. I deserve it. And I will savor every moment of it."

I lift my head so that she can read my face; so that she knows that I mean what I say from the bottom of my heart: "Mary, I know I don't have to tell you this, but I am anyway: you'll never have to do it again: covert operations —if you don't want to."

Mary nods slowly. "I know. To be honest, despite what Mario thinks—and even with all I pulled off this week—I don't really feel I'm cut out for field work. I'll make that very clear to Mario before we land. If he says I can't have the internship at the White House, so be it. Evan's offer still stands; that I work with him and his team on his top-secret project. And, now knowing how valuable it will be for our national defense, I'm honored he asked."

"He'll be lucky to have you on his team," I insist.

"He said the same thing. This time I know he meant it." She chuckles. "It's funny how being in the direst situation in the world with someone you truly care about will test the strength of your love. Well, not exactly 'funny-haha,' but...telling."

"It's why I trust your father completely. Even when... when he has to be intimate with another woman."

For a moment, my daughter's eyes remind me of my mother's, what with all the love and concern shining through them.

Mary's smile broadens. "Hey, you still want to do the mother-daughter survival week, right? After graduation?"

I chuckle. "Heck yeah!"

"Good. And let's make it count. Like, no holds barred."

"Ha! If you say so!"

"Yep, bring it on." She leans her head on my shoulder. "Because it's great to know that, should someone come after you, or Dad, or Trisha or Jeff—or Evan—I'd know what to do."

I understand.

It's what I've always wanted too.

"WHAT SMELLS SO GREAT?" I ASK.

The kitchen at Lion's Lair is a beehive of activity. All the noshing on the plane only whetted the appetites of Trisha's soccer team. The minute we got back to Lee's estate, the soccer team followed through on its boast to make a special treat for their host as a thank you for taking them on "such a fun trip!"

If only they knew how close they came to losing their beloved mascot.

Trisha is acting as the head chef, with Janie as her sous chef. The other girls are slicing and dicing fruit on their orders.

"It's that strawberry-banana-blueberry French Toast casserole recipe that Miss Delish whipped up right before the tournament." Trisha explains.

Aunt Phyllis pours a spoonful of maple syrup onto a large spoon, then sticks it into her mouth. Smacking her lips, she declares, "If it tastes as good as it looks, I might just let Trisha serve it at my rehearsal wedding brunch! It'll be perfect with mimosas." My aunt gives me a wink and whispers, "Of course, I'll have to watch how many mimosas I drink with it! Otherwise this bride will be blushing for all the *wrong* reasons!"

Trisha scoops me a plate of the casserole too.

I chew it thoughtfully. Then with a straight face, I say, "Wow! Miss Delish's is even better than mine."

Trisha raises her fist in victory. "I know! Divine, isn't it?" Sadly, she shakes her head. "I still can't believe she dropped out of the competition, leaving it to Grady McDougall to win!"

"Even Bake It or Fake It came up with better food combos," Janie chimes in. "Not that it matters now, what with FaceStaTweet out of the picture."

Ah! So, the girls know. "Yes, I heard it's offline," I murmur.

Trisha shrugs. "Frankly, I couldn't care less after watching first-hand how nasty some of those influencers were with their fans. Only Dominic was a sweetie. But then, we know that because he's like an uncle to me."

I gag on my French toast. "'*We know?*' Speak for yourself."

More like a *monkey's* uncle.

"That's okay. We like another platform much, much better," Trisha declares.

"It's called PinstaNote! Look!" Janie picks up her cell and starts clicking through it. "And, believe it or not, some of the influencers we already follow are there too."

"Oh, I believe it. Sort of like Whack-a-Mole," I grumble.

I feel my husband's arms around my waist. The girls giggle as his scratchy cheek nuzzles my neck. "What are you mumbling about?"

"Nothing that matters." I prove it with a kiss.

I mean it too. I can't get upset because there will always be other villains.

But there is only one Jack.

And only one Craig family.

Always and forever.

THE END

Other Books by Josie Brown

The Extracurricular Series

Books 1, 2, and 3

The Totlandia Series

The Onesies - Book 1 (Fall)

The Onesies - Book 2 (Winter)

The Onesies - Book 3 (Spring)

The Onesies - Book 4 (Summer)

The Twosies - Book 5 (Fall)

The Twosies – Book 6 (Winter)

The Twosies - Book 7 (Spring)

The Twosies - Book 8 (Summer)

The True Hollywood Lies Series

Hollywood Hunk

Hollywood Whore

More Josie Brown Novels

The Candidate

Secret Lives of Husbands and Wives

The Baby Planner

How to Reach Josie

To write Josie, go to:
mailfromjosie@gmail.com

To find out more about Josie, or to get on her eLetter list
for book launch announcements, go to her website:
www.JosieBrown.com

You can also find her at:

www.AuthorProvocateur.com

twitter.com / JosieBrownCA

facebook.com / josiebrownauthor

pinterest.com / josiebrownca

instagram.com / josiebrownnovels